LAST MINION STANDING

A Hell Story

EVE LANGLAIS

Copyright © January 2011 Eve Langlais

2nd edition © October 2015, Eve Langlais

Cover Art @May 2017 Dreams2Media

Produced in Canada

www.EveLanglais.com

ALL RIGHTS RESERVED

Last Minion Standing is a work of fiction and the characters, events and dialogue found within the story are of the author's imagination and are not to be construed as real. Any resemblance to actual events or persons, either living or deceased, is completely coincidental.

No part of this book may be reproduced or shared in any form or by any means, electronic or mechanical, including but not limited to digital copying, file sharing, audio recording, email and printing without permission in writing from the author.

eBook ISBN: 978-1-927459-86-7

Ingram ISBN: 978-1-77384-0178

CHAPTER ONE

A light bulb went on with a great big flash inside my head as brilliance struck.

"I need a minion," I announced.

My best friend, Jezebel, more commonly known as Jezzie, whom I'd grown up with in the hood known as Hell, looked up from her issue of *Demon's Duds* and frowned. "What do you need a minion for?"

Duh, like that wasn't totally obvious, but I explained anyhow. "If I'm going to be hunting down scummy souls and sending them back to Hell, then that kind of makes me a superhero, right?"

"I guess," said Jezzie slowly. "So why the need for a minion?"

"Don't all superheroes have a minion?" Redundant question, as I'd watched all the movies and had read like a zillion comic books—Batman had Robin,

Hercules was followed around by the weird satyr dude, Han Solo had Chewie. The pattern was clear. If I wanted fame—and the other side of the coin, fortune—I needed a lackey of my own, someone to enhance my natural awesomeness. Someone to poke at the crowd with a sharp stick if they failed to acknowledge my greatness. I could think of so many reasons to get myself a minion, including the fact that I'd grown tired of fetching my own coffee and dry cleaning.

Jezzie's face cleared in understanding, and she laughed. "I think those guys are called sidekicks."

Talk about splitting horns. I rolled my eyes. "Minion. Sidekick. Whatever you want to call it, I think I need one." Not just think, I knew I had to have one. Like yesterday.

"Sure, why not? I can see where a sidekick—"

"Minion."

"—might come in useful. But, if you're going to set yourself up as some kind of super crime fighter, shouldn't you have a cool name? I mean, seriously, even Diana Prince had a secret identity."

"Who is she?" The name drew a blank. I thought furiously. I knew who Clark Kent was, Peter Parker, too, but I'd never heard of this Diana broad. I eyed my smartphone and wondered if I could sneak a Google search. Then again, given Jezzie was watching me, waiting for an answer, probably not.

"Diana Prince." Jezzie sighed at my continued

blank look. "You know, Wonder Woman. Curvy bod. Awesome hair. She wore the American flag body suit and tiara."

That was enough of a clue for me to guess who Jezzie was talking about now. It was also enough for me to get a total hate-on for Diana because she not only already owned the best superhero name, she also had the sexiest supergirl outfit. "I know who she is, but talk about a mundane persona. Someone needs to hire a PR firm."

"Um, the whole point of a secret identity is to not have people find out."

"But then what's the point of being a superhero if not for the fame?"

"Doing the right thing? The thanks of the people?"

Altruism. Ugh. I'd take cold hard cash and front row tickets to concerts instead.

But back to the real problem at hand. Much as I hated to admit it, Jezzie had a good point. Somehow, my true name, Sally Jones, just didn't have an awe-inspiring ring or the right kind of syllables sure to make villains tremble. Totally my father's fault. He, a demon with the wicked and strong name of Asmodeus, had caved into the stupidest of human emotions—love. Ick. You wouldn't catch me falling in love. Lust yes, love never.

My father, though, had fallen hard for my mother and out of nostalgia for the human who begat me, he named me after her. I wasn't impressed. I might have felt differently if she'd lived to raise me, but all I had left of my mother, other than her name, were faded photographs.

"What do you think I should I call myself?" I asked, jumping from my sofa to pace back and forth. I really liked the idea of changing my name. "How about Sexy Lady? Or Wears Prada?"

Jezzie, the traitor who I'd demoted from best friend, laughed at my wonderful suggestions. I growled, and she laughed harder. It proved contagious, and I ended up joining in. Okay, so she might have a point. They weren't the greatest titles, but at least I'd gotten the ball rolling.

"I know what you should do," said Jezzie, the bright gleam in her eyes signaling the arrival of a great idea. I waited eagerly to hear it. Her last great idea had proven utterly fantastic and gotten us kicked out Hell for six months. I still wasn't allowed to talk about it according to the terms of the contract Satan made me sign. But damn, we'd had fun.

"Well, spit it out," I said. "Wait, don't spit. Last time your acid ate right through the carpet and floor into Mrs. Livingston's place, and she wasn't happy." For a human, my neighbor could be quite shrill.

"How about you have a contest?"

"A contest?" The suggestion percolated in my mind. "For a name or a minion?"

Bouncing on her knees, Jezzie clapped her hands. "Why not both? We'll setup a Hellbook fan page with pics of you doing superhero stuff and let the denizens of Hades choose your name. And, at the same time, we'll put out word we're accepting applications to become your sidekick."

"Minion," I corrected absently, my mind already turning this idea around in my head. Did I want strangers choosing my name? Then again, could they do any worse than I had so far? The more I thought of it, the more I liked it. "Let's do it." Words that, over the course of the years, had gotten Jezzie and me in countless trouble. Surely this time wouldn't be any different. I couldn't wait!

With a shout of glee, Jezzie dove for her laptop, and fingers flying, she got the proverbial ball rolling.

Leaving her tapping madly, I decided to pay a visit to the third bedroom in my condo, a space I'd converted into a walk-in closet. The room never failed to cheer me with its one wall taken up by a rack of shoes and boots. The other walls displayed clothing on hangers or folded neatly on shelves. Shopping wasn't just a fetish for me; it was an obsession, one that served me well because demon hunting wasn't just about the chase. It was totally about appearance too. And this had never been truer.

If I was going to be in the spotlight, dazzling the masses with my greatness, I'd need to dress the part. Of course, despite all the outfits and footwear I already owned, I managed to find nothing at all in my closet that would work. What a shame. I'd have to go shopping.

Stores beware. I grinned as I imagined my credit card screaming in my wallet.

CHAPTER TWO

A few hours later, I returned from a successful bout of shopping, laden with bags and not a single dime left on any of my credit cards. Overspending was a special talent of mine. Dropping the bags, I kicked off my heels and padded into the kitchen for a drink, only to spot my special phone from Hell flashing. In the shape of a pair of lips, it blinked red on and off to let me know someone had a mission for me. Tacky, but it was a gift from my daddy, so I made it work with the rest of my decor.

Before checking in, I peeked in on Jezzie, who absently waved at me, even as she still furiously typed. I mouthed, "Any luck?"

She gave me a thumbs-up that told me nothing.

The blinking phone taunted me, but I took a moment to put away my purchases. I hated wrinkles.

My new shoes, with the five-inch heels, looked divine. The leather pants were buttery smooth as I ran my hand down them. In short order, my purchases had a spot in their new home.

My pretties. My precious...

I'd stalled as long as I could. No longer able to avoid it, and knowing I was about to lose an evening of dancing and flirting, I returned to the kitchen and put the plastic lips to my ear before I pressed the only button on the base of the phone. The line rang a few times before someone answered.

"What do you want?" If it wasn't the snarky tone of my arch-nemesis, Medusa.

The serpentine-haired gorgon positively hated me. I think she resented the fact that I'd gotten to move topside, lived in a swanky apartment, and got to do all kinds of cool freaking stuff. It wasn't my fault she was stuck in Hell because she had an obvious head of snakes—although, I think her intense dislike of me might have also stemmed from the fact that I'd once braided her serpents when we were just kids. Some people just couldn't let go of the past.

"Hey, mouse breath," I said in a cheery voice. Did I forget to mention I still hadn't lost my instinct to drive her nuts?

"You." The disgust in her voice made me beam.

"Yes, it's me, your favorite soul hunter. What do you have for me today?"

"I heard about your contest, and I've got a suggestion for you."

Wow, Jezzie had truly worked hard in my absence if word was already getting around. "Oh yeah, let's hear it."

"Super Bubblehead." Medusa snorted in mirth, pleased with herself.

I tsked. "Really, Muddie, can't you come up with something more original? Bubblehead is so overdone already. If you're going to play, put a little effort into it, would you?"

The laughter on the phone stopped abruptly. "You've got a mission. This one is an escapee from Hell. Quite a nasty little fucker, too. I hope he gets you. Check your printer."

Without a chance to retort—a specialty of mine—Medusa cut the connection. As soon as she did, the printer I hid in the console table under the phone whirred to life. I opened the cabinet and pulled out the wanted poster that spat out into the tray, followed by a few fact sheets.

The Hell escapee didn't look too imposing—balding on top with a sharp nose, almost no chin, and beady eyes. The stats sheet put him at only five-foot-six, which was shorter than my barefoot five-foot-nine. I read his summarized bio.

Albert Jefferstein lived from 1898 to 1959. He killed over one hundred women, mutilating them while they were still alive. He was brought to Hell prema-

turely when one of the victim's mothers sold her soul in return for him being captured and punished eternally.

I perused the rest of the sheet, but mostly found an itemization of the crimes he'd committed and the punishment he'd incurred. I winced at what Albert had earned—Satan had a perverse sense of retribution. Do the crime, do the time. That was the big guy's motto. Many folks on the mortal plane had this mistaken idea that vile acts would earn them a special spot in Hell.

Wrong.

Satan had little sympathy or patience for criminals and murderers. Sure, he liked the occasional lie, a good fisticuff, and other things sure to earn you a spot in the pit, but he truly hated those who preyed upon the weak. Those bastards were sent to the toughest prison in Hell, where they were punished for eternity, unless they managed to get a pardon or escaped—escaped like Albert, my newest mission.

Something nagged at me, though. How had he escaped? Prisoners such as him, who received the most severe of punishments, were closely guarded. There was no way he could have escaped without help. I would have cared more except that wasn't my department, and I was sure my big boss, Satan, had noticed this glaring fact. The big man wouldn't tolerate incompetence. I could sense a television special coming where heads would roll, literally.

But back to the matter at hand—finding Albert.

Contrary to what Medusa and others thought, my job wasn't an easy one. Getting the lowdown on escapees didn't tell us where we'd find them nor help us seize them once we did. Anyone with the skills to escape Hell in the first place was a force to be reckoned with. A danger to humans and demons alike. It was a tough job, a dangerous one, and to everyone's surprise, I'd shown a knack for soul hunting.

My dad said I had intuition. I called it dumb luck. Either way, I was really good at finding the souls who had somehow fled Hell's punishments. And when it came to catching them, well, my years in the pit, where to get ahead you sometimes needed to kick some serious ass, had taught me some valuable fighting skills.

I read over the notes again, paying close attention to Albert's hometown and hunting ground, but I kept coming back to one nugget of info: the part describing the mother who'd sold her soul so Hell would take him early.

"Jezzie. I need the computer," I shouted, bringing my notes with me into the living room where she sat hunched over our laptop. Okay, her laptop, but we shared the apartment, so didn't that make her stuff my stuff? In my mind, it did. Of course, it didn't always work in the other direction, but Jezzie didn't seem to mind, most of the time anyway.

"Who are we looking for?" she asked, looking up. For those who've never met Jezzie, and trust me when I say you don't actually want to, she's a tiny thing. She barely comes up to my chin, with straight blonde hair, baby blue eyes, and the nastiest right hook your face ever met. Just ask the last demon who called her sweet thing. He'd drunk from a straw for weeks.

I gave her the name of the mother who'd sold her life and soul. "How many kids did she have?"

Jezzie did her magic, which involved hacking into databases that went beyond those the human government and police kept. Hell kept very thorough records of *everyone*. And yeah, that includes you. Don't think he's not watching your every move.

"Got it. She had one daughter who died at nineteen. They found her body mutilated. Another daughter lived and got married, but died of an aneurysm in her thirties."

"Did the living daughter have any kids before she croaked?" I was pretty sure I knew the answer already.

"Yes, one, a girl who is now twenty-one."

Bingo. "I need her location, please." And knowing the bureaucracy in Hell, it would be nearby because, even though they never gave me the answer, they always made sure to give soul retrieval missions to nearby bounty hunters.

I don't know if she Googled it, hacked it, or used arcane methods, but Jezzie found out where one Alice Smith, granddaughter to the mother who'd sold her soul, would be working tonight.

And just my luck, she was a bartender in a downtown dance club. It looked like I might get to go dancing—code speak for getting lucky—after all.

But first I had to find the perfect outfit for Lady Kickass. Okay, still not the right name, but I hadn't given up hope.

CHAPTER THREE

I paid the cab driver and stepped out onto the pavement across the street from the club where Alice worked. I stood in the shadows and surveyed the area, thinking. In or out? Where would Albert strike?

A long line of young, hot twenty-somethings stood in line waiting for the bouncer to give them the go-ahead to enter. Albert, with his looks, would never make it past the gorilla—I would, of course—but if Albert couldn't enter the club, where would he lurk in wait? His previous method of operation always had him attacking near the victim's place of work, hitting them when their shifts ended and they were headed home. Since I knew this, logic dictated I check the alley behind the club, which usually boasted an employee entrance. Dark and with less witnesses, it was a perfect spot for those wishing to indulge in nefarious activities, my favorite kind.

In this day and age, though, even the back doors were guarded against the unwanted, not a label that applied to me—humble I am not. Another gorilla of a bouncer leaned against the brick wall beside the employee entrance, smoking. If I'd wanted in, I would have just walked up to him and dazzled him with my presence, but I didn't want to go inside or be noticed. Besides, he wasn't my type. I liked big and muscled guys, but judging by his package, he lacked the heavy equipment needed for true satisfaction.

Not my fault I had specific needs. As a half-demon, I'd inherited some neat powers. I wasn't just gorgeous, awesome, and super sexy—not to mention completely shameless—I also had the ability to either be noticed or not, totally handy for the times when the situation called for a stakeout. But as a half-demon and daughter to a demon of lust, my sexual appetite went beyond voracious. I just thanked my lucky stars I'd inherited enough human to skip the succubus gene. The thought of draining a guy's soul while screwing him was a little too freaky, even for me.

Calling on my demonic abilities, I blended into the shadows and made my way to the gray metal doors that marked the back exit of the club. The thug in the black T-shirt didn't even look in my direction. Hidden, I performed the most boring aspect of my job. I waited.

Damn, I hated this part. The vibrations of the music blasting from the club thrummed through my body, calling me like a tempting siren—a male one, of course. It took a lot of willpower to keep my feet still, but I was on the job, so, hard as I found it, I bit my lip and persevered. I know, martyr material. Too bad the name Saint already belonged to someone. I could have really done something cool with that as my superhero name. A nun's habit with slits up the thigh and...

I left off imagining ways to sluttify a sister's holy dress when I heard the soft scuff of someone sneaking up the alley. The big brute at the rear door had just gone inside, and right on cue, out from the shadows, scuttled Albert, my escapee from Hell.

With my target in sight, I dropped my do-not-notice-me glamour—when I was young I used to like imagining I was part Jedi—and cranked up the look-at-me one on high. I strutted with swishing hips towards my target, my curvy frame undulating hypnotically. As expected, his eyes locked onto me, riveted by my sensuous motion. It would take a stronger soul than his to ignore my feminine attributes. I tried not to shudder when he licked his lips. His stay in Hell really hadn't agreed with him. I would describe his appearance, but trust me when I say you'd prefer to keep your cookies in your belly.

A few steps more, all that separated us, and I'd touch him. Then *wham*, I'd invoke the magic I got with the job. The spell would create a target-specific portal that would send Albert back to Hell where he belonged. Once he was in lockup, screaming his apologies for daring to flout the system, I'd collect the bounty for his capture. Some shoes I'd placed on layaway—because my cards were maxed out—were counting on this bonus.

At least that was the plan until *he* appeared. He dropped down from the night sky, an agile hunk of male who made my jaw drop for several reasons. One, he wore only a pair of indecently low-slung jeans, with no shirt and no shoes. I mean who came to a fight barefoot?

This simple fact distracted me and turned on my lust, which, in turn, annoyed me. Wasn't there an unwritten rule somewhere that stated, like most restaurants, shirts and shoes must be worn to a fight? If not, I'd start a lobby for one because the amount of naked—mmm, muscled—torso displayed was waaaaay too distracting for poor little me, who obviously hadn't received a good shag in a while.

The second thing that rendered me speechless—a state my dad would have found amusing—was the fact that Mr. Hunky bestowed upon me a masculine grin—a naughty one meant to make me cream my panties—and said in a velvety baritone, "Run along, sweetheart. I've got this."

Me, one of Hell's most successful bounty hunters, dismissed with a smile and a wave of his hand. His treatment made me want to tear his pants off and ride him like a cowgirl—I mean, he'd called me sweetheart, how hot was that?—while, at the same time, made me see red.

I'm gonna wipe the smirk off his face. Then I'm gonna kiss him. Then...

Caught in so many conflicting emotions, I'm afraid I didn't react quickly enough, and he took matters into his own hands. Did I mention they were huge? He turned and gave me his back, which, I'll admit, was almost as sexy as his front and would have only been improved with a set of nail marks—mine, of course. With an animalistic grace that would have put most predators to shame, Mr. Creams-Panties approached my target and engaged him in a slugfest.

What a show. I totally needed a fan or, even better, a really cold ice pack for my crotch. Heat suffused me as I watched Mr. Cream dance around a dazed-looking Albert. I'd forgotten all about the bounty in my fascination with watching him move. In that moment, I was just like a man, lust making all the blood in my brain rush to other places, and I think I might have drooled.

The hunk used no weapon, unlike the scuzzball Albert, who wielded a serrated knife, a dangerous fact that did not daunt my shoeless hero in the least. His fists flashed and connected with solid thumps. The escaped soul reeled beneath the force of his blows, but no matter how well my hero acquitted himself, he couldn't win. Souls couldn't die.

Sucking in my stomach—scrawny I was not—I strutted over to interfere and send the wandering one back to Hades. I looked forward to collecting my reward for a job well done, and as a treat for Mr.

Cream being hot, I'd bestow some of my pleasure on the treasure hidden in his pants.

Before I could touch Albert and say the words to send him back where he belonged, my shirtless wonder said them, and with a dwindling scream of frustration —a scream I almost repeated—my new pair of shoes, umm target, was sucked back to Hell.

I gaped at the glistening skin on the back of my shirtless hunk, too angry for words—not to mention still hornier than ever.

He turned and faced me. With a sensual smile, he strutted toward me, and even in my pissed-off state, I couldn't help the arousal that flashed through me. He was fucking gorgeous. Built like an ox and at least six and a half feet, he towered over me. Slabs of muscle covered his impossibly wide chest, and his arms were so thick I doubted I could get both hands around them. His skin was tanned and smooth while his unruly hair was black as night. Fuck me, I wanted him—naked, like right now.

A light glinted in his shockingly blue eyes, and I wondered briefly what demon caste he belonged to, for this close, I could sense his *otherness*.

I said nothing when he placed a hand around my waist and pulled me hard against him, lifting me so our lips aligned. Another kind of girl might have protested his manly assumption. That girl wasn't me.

I wanted him to kiss me. And he did.

The touch of his hard lips on mine sent an electric

shock throughout my body, and I clutched at him tightly as my knees turned to pudding and buckled. His mouth slanted over mine, claiming it with seductive mastery. Lest you think I completely succumbed to him, I should note I gave back as good as I got, slipping my tongue between his lips to wetly tangle with his.

I lost myself in the pleasure of the kiss. Unlike many prudes, I saw no issue with making out with guys I barely knew. I tended to live in the moment, and boy, this was one moment I didn't want to end.

Plastered against his solid length, I couldn't miss his erection as it pulsed against me behind the confining material of his jeans. I ground myself against it, and he grunted in my mouth. He slid his hands down from my waist to cup my full ass and pressed me more firmly against him.

Oh sweet fucking bliss. Wet didn't come close to describing the state of my pussy, and I couldn't wait to soak his cock.

If it hadn't been for the stupid drunken humans who came stumbling into the alley, I would have screwed him, right there against the brick wall. But I had a softer bed at my place. We separated, our breathing uneven, pulses racing, and I opened my mouth to tell him to come back to my apartment so I could make him a lucky man.

He, unfortunately, spoke first and ruined my mood. "You're welcome."

I think my jaw dropped. I know I clenched a fist when I asked him tightly, "Welcome for what?"

"Rescuing you, of course."

I gaped at him then I lost it. "Listen here, you—you—" I sputtered.

"Drake."

Ooh, hot name, but I wouldn't let his hotness distract me from my anger, lusty hormones or not. "I don't know who you think you are, but I had things perfectly under control until you decided to jump out of the sky like some underdressed Batman and take over. That was my bounty you stole."

He scoffed at me, and I let it pass. I know. I was surprised I didn't kill him too.

"Please, a cute little thing like you a bounty hunter?"

I restrained myself from preening. Me, cute and little? Damned smooth talker. But pretty words wouldn't allow him to escape my wrath. "Don't you use flattery to cloud the issue. I was assigned this bounty by the Hellacious Office of Escapees." More shortly known as HOE.

He crossed his arms over his impressive chest, and my mouth went dry because all the moisture in my body headed straight for my pussy.

"Impossible. They put me on this case just today."

Even though I was slightly overcome with lust, things suddenly became clear. "Medusa," I snarled. "I'm gonna feed her snakes laxatives for this."

A rumbling chuckle made me break off from the swearing and various tortures I'd inflict on the slithery bitch. "What's so damned funny?" I asked, features creased in a scowl, one that I might add didn't intimidate him at all.

"You're funny. And cute when you're mad." His eyes glinted with mirth, and his lips twitched in a smile that made me want to taste them all over again. "Say, do you want to get a coffee or *something*?"

Ha, first he'd stolen my bounty, and then he thought I was going to let him ravish me. Hmm, then again, on second thought, a ravishment that included a lot of oral would probably go a long way toward appeasing me.

"I say let's skip right to the something." I grabbed his hand and pulled him toward the street where we could flag a cab. I could have called a portal, but I really had this thing for making out in the backseat of cabs while the driver watched.

I didn't drag my shirtless hunk for long, as his greater stride brought him alongside me and his fingers weaved through mine, an intimate gesture I wouldn't have believed of a big guy like him.

"I don't suppose you'll tell me your name before you have your way with me?" he asked, humor in his tone. "I'm Drake by the way."

"So you already said. I'm Sally," I replied absently, looking up the street for a yellow taxi.

"Wait a second." He halted and turned me to face him. "You wouldn't be *the Sally* would you?"

"Depends. Which Sally are you talking about?"

"The one I heard about. The one who's put up a page on Hellbook looking for a superhero name and a sidekick."

"Minion," I corrected.

He laughed. I didn't get the joke, so I stood there tapping my foot, glaring at him, my ardor shriveling with each guffaw. He kept howling, though, so I finally had to ask. "What's so fucking funny?"

"I expected someone bigger and badder," he snorted, "not some cute little thing. And it's not a sidekick you need, but a boyfriend to take care of you."

He had not seriously just said that. "I don't need a man to take care of me. I do fine on my own." I stepped away from him.

"Ah, don't be mad. I think it's adorable you're looking for help. I'm here if you want to give me a test run." He shot me a charming smile.

I deflected it with a shield of pride. My chin angled. "I don't think so, and when it comes to the position of minion or boyfriend, you need not apply. And as for not being bad enough for my job, let me show you why I'm not a girl you fuck with." I wear pointy-toed shoes for a reason, and I showed Drake one of their many painful uses.

A cab pulled up as he hunched over gasping for air. I smiled at him sweetly. "Next time, hands off my escapee. And in the future, wear a shirt. It's indecent for you to gallivant around half-naked, distracting those of us with serious jobs to do."

I could have sworn I heard him laugh as I slammed the cab door shut. Not likely, only a madman would find humor in the pain I'd inflicted.

Turns out he was somewhat masochistic.

CHAPTER FOUR

Drake, hunched and wheezing from the radiating pain in his balls, somehow still found the breath to laugh.

Damn, what a woman.

Only rarely did he meet a female who didn't either swoon at his looks or cower at his size. And while he'd seen the admiration in Sally's eyes—and tasted it in her kiss—he hadn't intimidated her at all, a fact that his inner beast noticed and approved of. Actually, his beast more than liked this girl. It wanted him to go after the ballsy Sally and...*claim her?*

Drake stopped dead en route to his apartment. No way. Surely he misunderstood.

Or not. His beast stirred and whispered sibilantly in his mind. *Mark her. Claim her. She is our mate.*

Oh hell no. Drake shook his head in negation and resumed walking, but the idea he'd found the one woman who could complete him churned in his mind. *And all I know so far about her is her name is Sally and she's a bounty hunter for Hell.* Oh, and he shouldn't forget the fact that someone wanted her discredited, or worse, from the soul retrieval game.

When he'd accepted the job to steal a bounty out from a hunter's nose, he hadn't asked questions, not with the zeros attached to the fee. Nor had he batted an eye at the postscript that stated there would be a bonus if the original hunter for slimy Albert got hurt or killed. The games played by the denizens of Hell were both varied and deadly, and in this demon-eat-demon world, only the strongest survived. *Like me.*

As one of the stronger players, he had a choice. He could dispatch the lovely Sally and collect the money—his hoard could always use more riches—or he could ignore one treasure in order to claim a bigger one. Her.

The answer was already clear. If he'd wanted the bonus dollars, he could have easily dispatched her in the alley. But he hadn't. And he wouldn't.

While it would seem Sally had been unknowingly drawn into a game of survival, she had a hidden advantage—*Me.* Which begged the question, what where the rules, and who were the opposing players? Something he'd have to discover if he was to keep her safe until he could claim her.

Funny how the very idea didn't make him panic. For a man set in his bachelor ways, he was awfully calm about the fact that he'd met the one woman who would complete him. Then again, hadn't he waited centuries to find *the one?*

The humans called it love at first sight. Drake called it fate. Fate had drawn them together, and fate would bind them, if she lived long enough.

Someone wanted her dead.

His inner beast growled. *Danger. We must protect her.*

Drake got the feeling Sally could protect herself, but that wouldn't stop him from finding out more about the sexy lady and who seemed bent on destroying her. And once he found the one who thought to hurt his mate, he'd first thank them for introducing him to the woman who would soon grace his bed, and then he would rip their head from their body and bathe in his enemy's blood.

Shocked? Too bad. This was who he was. Inside, his darker side chuffed in anticipation.

CHAPTER FIVE

Muttering under my breath, I stalked into my apartment in a high dudgeon. "Stupid, too-hot-for-his-own-good asshat."

"Ooh, sounds like I missed out. What happened?" asked Jezzie. She emerged from the kitchen munching on some chips.

I needed them more than she did so I snatched the bag from her hands and flounced over to the couch, where I collapsed. It took several handfuls of sour cream and onion crunchiness before I could tell her the events of the evening.

The bitch laughed. "Damn. I wish I'd been there. You kicking his balls up into his stomach would have made an awesome video for your fan page."

Who cared about a video? The man had dissed me. Treated me like I was a...girl. Ugh.

I stuffed another handful of chips in my mouth.

Some women turned to chocolate in times of stress, I preferred salty goodness, and if I couldn't indulge in the bedroom variety, then the crunchy, out-of-a-bag kind would do.

"Speaking of fan pages, did you know we already have over five thousand followers? You're a hit."

The news perked my irritated spirt. "Really?"

Jezzie bobbed her head. "We've also got tons of names for you to check out and even a few applications for the sidekick position. Now, I was thinking." Ooh, dangerous. "Interviews seem like a piss-poor way to test your new sidekick's mettle. It occurred to me what we really should do, instead, is make them accomplish some tasks. Things to show they're the right fit for you. That they can understand and predict your needs."

"Like fetching my coffee and making sure it's the right temperature with just the right amount of cream," I added helpfully.

"No. Harder stuff. Television-worthy shit. My buddy over at HBC says this would make a perfect reality miniseries, and we've already hashed out the contracts."

HBC, Hell's Broadcasting Corporation, talk about the big times. "Me? On television?" Hot damn. I'd need to go shopping again.

Jezzie went over the details of the contract with me and gave me the knife to prick my finger. Hell's bureaucracy didn't rely on unreadable signatures to seal contracts. Nothing but one-of-a-kind blood would do. As to the show itself, basically, I needed to do nothing. No lines to memorize or scripts to follow. Without me even being aware of it, cameras would trail me and the contestants selected to compete for the position of minion. I'd have to make sure I looked my best at all times. I also really hoped they hadn't taped this evening's fiasco.

How was I supposed to get any respect when Drake—with his bare chest and big muscles—insisted on treating me like a fragile damsel?

Now if only my body would stop humming in excitement at his actions and words.

At least I had the HBC deal to distract me from Drake. I went to bed excited about becoming a television star, but I tossed and turned as a certain muscular somebody kept interrupting my thoughts of fame and fortune.

Attraction to a male wasn't a new feeling for me. Thinking about him, though, after I'd left his presence? I couldn't remember that happening before.

Love 'em and leave 'em—I'd grown up faithfully following our family motto. My longest relationship with an incubus—my blood protected me from their soul sucking, that or I had no soul—lasted less than a month, a record for me.

I tried thinking about anyone else, even the superhot Damon character from the television show *The Vampire Diaries*, but over and over, the rugged face and body of Drake superimposed itself over my usual fantasy figures. Maybe it was because he'd left me horny. I needed some kind of explanation for why I couldn't help remembering Drake's muscular body as he'd slugged it out with the escaped soul. His smooth, tanned skin that I still, even after his obnoxious behavior, wanted to lick.

Lick. Touch. Rub...

Shuddering in arousal, I gave in to my libido and pulled open the drawer to my nightstand. I pulled out "Bob," the boyfriend who never disappointed me. Long and hard, his black rubber length was just the thing I needed to sate my pussy tonight. I dripped some oil on his rubbery length then rubbed the bulbous head across my clit, but while it felt good, I needed more.

Closing my eyes, I pictured Drake, his chest slick with sweat, his dark hair rumpled and his blue eyes smoky with desire. My sex flooded with wetness, eager for more.

I wondered how his cock looked. Long and lean or thick and juicy? Would he fuck me fast or torture me with long, deep strokes? I worked my rubber phallus into my sex, sliding it in and out, my thoughts of Drake exciting me, but my orgasm hung just out of reach. A rubber substitute just couldn't take the place of the real thing.

Frustrated and beyond aroused, I pushed faster, my breath coming in pants. But when my cell phone rang, satiation slipped away.

Cursing technology but wondering who could be

calling at this hour, I let go of Bob—after all it wasn't as if I was getting anywhere—and grabbed my cell. A glance at the display showed a number I didn't recognize. Maybe, if I was lucky, it would be an obscene caller who'd have suggestions on how I could get off.

I answered in my sexiest phone sex voice. "Hello."

"Are you touching yourself?"

At the query, I almost dropped the phone in shock. I hadn't actually expected a naughty caller. Things were looking up. "Who is this?" I asked.

"I can't stop thinking of you," my anonymous caller replied instead. "I wanted you to know that, even though you did your best to turn me into a eunuch, I have recovered and I'm stroking my big cock right now."

My eyes widened, and even in my shock over him calling, my pussy began to throb. "Drake? Is that you? How did you get my number?"

"I have my ways. But you never answered my question. Are you touching yourself?"

I thought for maybe a nanosecond about hanging up, but as usual, my hormones did my thinking, and instead, I put him on speakerphone and placed my cell on the pillow beside me.

"I'm naked," I told him huskily. "And very, very wet."

Drake groaned. "Oh, baby. You are so fucking hot. Squeeze your tits for me and pinch your nipples."

Forget my earlier irritation. His words were totally

what I needed right now. I wasn't ashamed to admit having him give me orders of a sexual kind excited me. I grabbed my breasts and eagerly obeyed. Since I found myself already aroused, this touching on his command just heightened my pleasure, and I moaned.

"Just so you know, babe, I've got my hand around my cock. It's so fucking thick and hard right now. I'm imagining it between your tits, the tip of my shaft touching your lips."

My hand found Bob, and I slid him between my breasts, which I pushed together. I licked the tip, imagining it was a real pulsing rod, Drake's rod.

"What are you doing?" he asked in a gravelly voice.

"I've got my dildo between my tits, and I'm sucking it," I answered honestly.

"Fuck." The expletive was followed by some heavy breathing. "You're going to make me lose control, babe. Put your dildo between your legs. I want you to rub it against your clit. It's what I intended to do to you tonight. I was going to rub your little nubbin with my cock until you squirmed and juiced yourself."

His words painted a vivid picture, and I almost came, especially when I rubbed my rubber toy against my clit. I closed my eyes and pictured Drake above me, his thick prick poking at me as I arched my hips, begging for him to fuck me. Faster, I frictioned my swollen nub, my breath coming fast.

"Tell me what you want," he growled.

"I want you to fuck me," I panted. "Slide your cock into my pussy and fuck me hard."

"Yes," he hissed. "I'm inside your sweet pussy now. Can you feel me, pounding you?"

I slammed my dildo in and pumped myself hard. "Yes," I cried. "Harder."

He didn't speak, just grunted, and I mewled as I slammed my phallus in and out.

"Come for me," he said in a strained voice.

And I did, keening as my channel, with a mighty quiver, finally crossed the edge into pleasure. Blissful waves made my sex contract hard, and I cried out with each pulse. I heard Drake shout as he found his own release.

Finally sated, I slid my dildo out of my happily throbbing pussy and grabbed the phone. "Thank you for calling Sally's phone sex service," I said in a sultry tone. "Expect a bill for thirty-nine ninety-five. Bye."

Then I hung up. Great phone sex didn't mean I forgave him his laughter. He'd have to work harder to gain my forgiveness. On his knees, sucking my pussy, for starters.

With a smile, I went to sleep.

CHAPTER SIX

DRAKE GRINNED AS HE HUNG UP THE PHONE. Talking to Sally—and masturbating together—was well worth the favor he'd cashed in with his buddy over at HOE. He'd also used another IOU to dig up all the information available about the woman he'd soon take as mate.

Their eventual joining was just a matter of time. Fighting it would just delay the inevitable, and besides, it looked as if his beast had chosen well. She embodied everything he loved in a woman from her long dark hair, perfect for pulling on, to her luscious, curvy frame made to cushion a man's body. Correction, his body. He got the impression life would never be boring with Sally around—and the sex? Cataclysmic. Drake's cock stirred.

As a shifter, part of his heritage included the fact that, when he least expected, he'd encounter his mate, the one who would complement him and his beast. Drake never imagined he'd find his so soon, but having met the sexy Sally, he couldn't wait to make her his, a sentiment his beast growlingly echoed.

He'd found the background info on her very interesting, especially the parts blacked out with "Classified" stamped over them. From the sounds of the sections he could read, she was one tough cookie capable of dishing it out. She also harbored a naughty streak judging by some of her escapades, those that hadn't been censored. He—and his beast—really liked her naughty side, and he looked forward to tasting it firsthand.

Flipping on the television to distract him before he called her again for another round of phone sex, he first checked out the human channels, but other than infomercials and the weather network, there wasn't much to watch. He hit the special button on his remote and tuned to HBC. To his disbelieving eyes, the object of his lust appeared. Muttering to his beast to shut up, he turned up the volume.

"Do you have what it takes to become this stunning lady's sidekick? Imagine working daily in close proximity to this goddess of latex, her every wish your desire. Only the strongest, brightest, and slyest need apply. First round in the elimination is..."

Drake listened to the rest of the broadcast before he turned off the television. He got up and paced. When he'd heard about the Hellbook posting of Sally looking for a superhero name and sidekick, he'd easily laughed it off; after all, new groups popped up daily on HB and never went anywhere. But someone had latched onto Sally and her quest, pushing her into the spotlight, where males of all kinds could drool and compete to work closely with her. Not to mention, whoever wanted her hurt or out of the soul retrieval game would not be happy at her newfound fame, probably painfully so. Drake growled, even before his beast had a chance to.

She's mine. I must protect her, even from herself. What to do though? She'd probably signed contracts to abide by the terms of the contest, and knowing Hell's lawyers, the consequences of breaking them would be severe. Which left only one alternative.

He'd have to compete. And win.

Then claim...

CHAPTER SEVEN

When I finally dragged my ass out of bed at the indecent hour of two p.m., it was to discover Jezzie had turned our living room into a war zone. I rubbed bleary eyes and looked again. Nope, still a fucking war zone.

"What's with all this?" I asked Jezzie as she bustled from the laptop to the large whiteboards propped all over the place and covered in arcane scrawls.

"This board is name suggestions," she said, pointing. "And this one is for sidekick applications."

I rubbed my eyes, but the scene didn't change. The scrolling amount of names applying for the job of my minion was staggering. "I can't screen all those guys. They are guys, right? I don't want any girls trying to steal my limelight."

Jezzie snapped her fingers, and a quarter of the names on the board disappeared. "Done. I'll adjust the online application. As for the rest, I've got the first round of eliminations scheduled for this afternoon."

"So soon?" I squeaked. My innocent statement of needing a minion had taken on a life of its own and was now barreling like a giant snowball down a steep hill. Weeee! Other people might fear chaos and the limelight. I embraced it.

"Don't worry. All you need to do is show up. I've got everything else under control."

"Exactly what I'm afraid of," I muttered as I went in search of caffeine. After having slept on it, I wasn't so sure I wanted a minion anymore. Actually, I found myself in the mood for one shirtless and shoeless man instead. He had a pair of low-hipped pants just begging for a pair scissors so I could see if he wore boxers, briefs, or, even better, nothing at all.

While a happy Jezzie went completely overboard in her quest to help me, I showered and dressed for a visit to Hell. First stop, the HOE's offices and Medusa—my fist really wanted to chat with her mouth.

Two hours later, and only because I rushed to get ready, I strutted into the HOE office building like I owned it, my indecently high heels clacking loudly on the polished floor. I knew I looked hot, having dressed in a red leather mini with a jet-colored blouse tied off just underneath my boobs while an elastic held my hair up in a high ponytail, the strands long enough to tickle my waist. I called that hairstyle the Tomb Raider, for it was just like the one Angelina Jolie wore in the movie.

I just wished I had her perfectly plump lips—and Brad Pitt. Sigh.

Back to business. I made my way up to the dispatch office to have a few *friendly* words with my nemesis, Medusa. I wouldn't tolerate the crap she'd pulled on me the day before. I intended to make very clear the future consequences should she decide to repeat her unprofessional behavior.

What I hadn't expected to find was Drake already perched on Medusa's desk, his head bent low as he whispered something to her, a certain something that made her blush and laugh.

My irritation rose, and I scowled, not because I was jealous, or because he wore a shirt over his magnificent bod, but because I could see my threats about to fall on deaf ears. I'd take bodily harm over pleasing the hot guy any day, and I figured Medusa, who didn't get many chances at a hottie of his caliber, wouldn't even bat an eye. I restrained myself from kicking things in frustration.

Medusa chose that moment to notice me, and she did so with a smirk. "If it isn't the Big Hoe herself."

"Jealous?" I smiled and added an extra wiggle to my walk when I noticed Drake's eyes raking me from head to toe. "Oh, and Big Hoe is copyrighted to the president of the succubus union. Do your homework."

The cap of snakes on Medusa's head danced and hissed in agitation. "Let me guess, you're here to bitch about the mishap with last night's takedown?" Now, some girls might have smacked the smirk off her face, but I was much more devious than that.

I threw a sultry look at Drake. "Why would I bitch when that little booboo meant me getting to meet this great big hunk of man? On the contrary, I actually want to thank you for making my evening so *pleasurable.*"

Medusa's lips tightened, so much they almost welded completely shut. With a wink at Drake, I sashayed back to the elevators. I should have known he'd follow me. Actually, I'd hoped he would.

Ignoring him wasn't easy in the close confines of the elevator. Especially when he hit the stop button and I found myself pressed up against the mirrored wall. Thick arms bracketed me, and I angled my chin so I could peek at him through thick lashes.

"What are you doing?" I asked.

"Saying hello," was his reply before his scorching lips found mine in a kiss that made me swoon. I clutched his broad shoulders for a moment, allowing the pleasure his touch ignited to sweep through me.

But I had no intention of making this too easy for him, good phone sex or not. My sharp teeth nipped at his lip and drew blood. He pulled his head back and regarded me with glowing eyes. Why his eyes kept glowing around me was a mystery, but the fact that his did almost made me grab his head to drag him back in for another smooch. However, I had places to be, minions to judge, and millions of viewers waiting to watch my awesome self.

"Now that you've said hello, we need to say goodbye. I've got an appointment."

"Meet with me later." His husky voice tickled my skin with awareness.

A part of me wanted to dive back on him for another kiss, maybe more. But no. I had to stay strong. And I meant strong, seeing as how it was an effort to say, "Sorry, sweetcheeks, but I'll have to pass." I patted him on the side of his smooth-shaven jaw. "While you are a hot piece of ass, my schedule is quite busy for the next little bit."

He moved back and leaned against the opposite wall, and his lips tilted in a half-smile. "Ah yes, the contest for sidekick."

"I'm glad you understand. Maybe in a few weeks, when things calm down, you can give me a call." The brushoff, a classic. This was where I'd find out just how interested he was in me. I loved being chased—and getting fucked, um, I mean caught.

Since he didn't seem ready to press the issues—or any other parts of my body, the jerk—I jabbed the button to resume the elevator's descent.

He said not a word in reply, but his eyes watched me, and I restrained an urge to squirm under his intent scrutiny. Good thing I'd worn panties today because they caught the seeping moisture his mere presence caused. While I might hide the evidence of my arousal, he, on the other hand, couldn't hide the bulging erection in his jeans. A very impressive bulge. For me.

My mouth watered, and I swallowed with disappointment—saliva just wasn't the same as fresh cream.

"See you around." I waved with false cheer as I exited the elevator, a little annoyed when he didn't reply or follow.

No matter. I had more important things to attend to, and I definitely didn't feel bummed when he didn't try to trail me or convince me to get better acquainted. What a tease.

Miffed—and annoyingly aroused—I made my way to Hell's coliseum. Slowly, I managed to change my focus from Drake to the upcoming reality show. It still blew my mind it was happening. I mean, look at everything Jezzie had accomplished in such a short time.

As I neared the giant coliseum, I slowed my step, and not just because the massive height of the stone block structure inspired awe. It did. I mean, who wouldn't be impressed by the number of battles and contests and concerts that had graced this venue? But it wasn't those memories of the times I'd stripped my shirt, screamed my lust, and tossed my bra at the lead singer that made me stop and stare. It was the crowd.

A stream of demons and damned went through the various entrances. and I wondered if I'd gotten the time wrong for my own appearance. Surely they couldn't all be here for my first minion elimination round?

But as it turned out, they were, at least according to the snippets of conversation I heard.

"There she is. Wow, she's even hotter in person."

"I wouldn't mind being her sidekick, if you know what I mean."

"Think if I'm bad, she'll come punish me?"

I preened under the comments. I also smiled and waved as more and more heads began to turn and hands pointed. I could have done without the ass slaps and pinches, though. I'd have bruises tonight for sure.

I spotted Jezzie's familiar pigtails bobbing at the main entrance and headed toward her.

"What's up with the crowd?" I said.

"I told you this thing was taking off." Jezzie beamed. "Now come on, we've got to get you ready for your first official appearance."

A group of vultures, who claimed official positions like hair and makeup, attacked me when we reached the bowels of the coliseum. The clothes I'd chosen were torn from my body, and I found myself clad in a red latex suit meant to leave little to the imagination—kind of like most of my wardrobe actually.

Jezzie wisely stayed out of reach—smart demon, for had she gotten close enough, I would have wrung her neck. I'd gone past snowball. This had turned into a hurricane, and its gale force now flung me around like a rag doll. Before I could say, "Boo"—although I managed to exclaim "Fuck" a few times—I found myself behind a blood-red curtain on stage.

I looked to the wings on my left and mouthed at Jezzie. "What the fuck do I do now?"

"Just follow the emcee's lead."

Emcee? Sure enough, I heard a booming voice on the other side of the silken barricade.

"Good afternoon, denizens of Hell. Are you ready for the first round in *Last Sidekick Standing*?"

A roar met his words, and if my feet hadn't been frozen as if stuck in heavy cement shoes, I would have run, really, really far.

Instead, my mouth got dry, my hands clammy, and when the curtain suddenly pulled away, the bright lights blinded me. I made a mental note to place an ad looking for a new roommate because the one I had was going to die shortly. Cowardice thankfully didn't run in my family, though. I sucked in my stomach and smiled. The crowd cheered.

Their adulation helped me regain a bit of my equilibrium. But having not prepared a speech, I faked it. "Yo, friends and enemies of Hell, I am glad you got your asses here because, as you've probably heard, I need a minion."

"Sidekick!" someone out of sight hissed.

My elevated middle finger to the idiot daring to interfere with my awesome speech was met with cheers. Ha. The crowd loved me, and I relaxed.

"As a bounty hunter for Hell, tasked with dragging back the most vile of escapees, I find myself in need of a minion, someone capable of enhancing my greatness and aiding me on my quest to make money so I can buy shoes." The female component of the crowd went wild. Would you look at that? I was a natural at this. "But not just any minion will do. He must be the best of the best. The hottest of the hottest. Today we're going to test some of the applicants and see if they have what it takes." Unsure of what they had planned—no one had deigned to inform me—I raised an arm and lowered it, shouting, "Let the games begin."

Stamping, clapping, and whistling made the stage shiver. What a rush. Without my noticing, a throne appeared behind me. Sweet. I sat in the monstrous chair and waited with bated breath like everyone else to see what would happen next.

Like the Roman coliseum of old, the stadium seating and stage surrounded an inner open area with massive, iron-bound doors ringing it. Mere mortals would have cringed to hear about some of the famous bloody events that had played out here over the centuries. It also featured great acoustics for concerts.

The doors of the arena opened, and an eye-popping amount of half-clad men and demons came rushing out. My jaw dropped. Surely not all of these males wanted the position of minion. Talk about flattering. And hot.

Indecent amounts of bare flesh ran around hacking and slashing in a free-for-all, cheered on by a blood-thirsty crowd.

Some of the contenders sported weapons like

swords and knives, a few flailed whips, some resorted to their bare fists, and others just used themselves, which, in the case of demons and shapeshifters, could be deadlier than any weapon forged.

Riveted, I watched as sweaty, muscled bodies slugged and kicked. Talk about an early birthday present way better than any strip club. Before long, I found my eyes caught by one particular figure—a familiar one. Surely it couldn't be.

I leaned forward and didn't know whether I should curse or cheer, for flattening a goodly amount of applicants was Drake. Once again shoeless and shirtless, his body gleamed with perspiration, and his muscles rippled as he competed. Despite my irritation with his treatment of me, I found myself silently cheering him.

I couldn't have said how long the all-out brawl lasted, but when it came down to five males still standing, a bell rang, and the fighting stopped.

A flurry of minor demons flew into the ring and cleared the groaning, bleeding, and, in some cases, unconscious bodies out of the way. The five remaining contestants formed a line in front of me, and I got a chance to see who had prevailed in this first vicious round.

The tallest by at least a half foot was a demon with grey/green skin. His short horns and clear skin indicated his youth. Beside him stood a wolfman who, as I watched, shifted back into his human form, a very naked male body with an impressive package that made the females in the crowd titter. Then there was some kind of lizard dude, whose yellow slitted eyes and forked tongue totally freaked me out. The fourth player was a guy with a thick, squat body and a ton of facial hair, which made me think he was of dwarfish origin. Interesting, for their kind rarely ventured forth. Finally, looking tastier than a caramel-covered cheesecake, Drake.

The emcee's voice boomed. "And out of the hundred, we are left with five tough enough to continue on in the battle for the title of *Last Sidekick Standing*. Tomorrow, we shall test their cunning. My lady with no name, would you like to give us some parting words?"

Taken by surprise, I blurted out the first thing that came to mind. "I think I need a drink."

Apparently, I'd said the right thing because my words were met with a roar of approval, and to my relief, the curtain came crashing down. I stalked off the stage looking for Jezzie, but she'd disappeared, the sneaky bitch.

Tired, hungry, and needing a stiff drink—not to mention aroused—I opened a portal back to my apartment. I vaguely wondered what the test of cunning on the morrow would entail, but couldn't think further than my hunger. One food wouldn't satisfy. Turned out my appetite craved something more carnal, say a Drake sausage smothered in my bun.

Drake. Drake. Drake. My thoughts kept turning

back to him. And with good reason. It wasn't just the kisses that occupied my mind.

I can't believe he's competing. Is this his way of getting closer to me? Surprise didn't come close to explaining my emotions when I'd seen him competing to be mine.

Mine. Snicker. I needed to remind myself this wasn't *The Bachelorette*. Yet, at the same time, given Drake's earlier chuckle over the contest, I found it flattering he'd decided to participate. Could his actions be considered courting? And was it wrong for me to mentally root for him? After all, I hadn't actually met the other contestants.

Fuck all the thinking. What I needed was to blow off some steam, and since I refused to call Drake for some horizontal tango action, the next best thing to burn some of this excess energy was dancing.

First, though, I needed a shower where I could get intimate with my detachable sprayer. In my opinion, every girl should have one for her cleansing pleasure.

CHAPTER EIGHT

Dressed to kill, literally, with knives strapped to my thighs under my miniskirt and needles in my upswept hair, I went dancing. I would have taken Jezzie along, because I never could stay mad at my best friend for long, but she claimed she needed to work on the next day's competition. I briefly thought of helping her, but honestly, if I didn't blow off some steam, I'd probably snap, and not in a good way. The last time I'd let stress get to me, it had taken gallons of cold water and bleach to clean the stains.

But I did feel better afterwards. Seeing as how humans tended to frown upon killing—spoilsports—I knew working off my tension was the less complicated solution.

For some reason, I ended up returning to the club of the previous night, where I'd met Drake for the first time. I'd never gotten to check the inside out, what with all the distractions going on, so I found myself curious.

The lineup outside didn't daunt me. My super-wet lip-gloss and the twenty I slipped the bouncer ensured my prompt entry into the thumping building. The DJ apparently enjoyed a deep beat, for I could feel the bass, like a heartbeat, vibrating throughout my body.

Hips leading the way, I gyrated my way onto the dance floor, where I closed my eyes and let myself go to the wild rhythm. As usual, when I became one with the music, I attracted attention. Bodies, both male and female, brushed against me. I didn't bother looking. It was the same everywhere I went. Even with my power turned off, as soon as my hips got going, humans just couldn't resist me.

I don't know how long I swayed and gyrated, but I suddenly noticed the mortals brushing against me moving away, and I could have sworn I heard a thump and a grunt as the guy dirty dancing against my ass abruptly disappeared. A new body took his place and moved in time with me, a firm body that sent a familiar tingle through me.

Instant heat flooded me, and I didn't need to turn around to know who rubbed against my backside.

Drake.

A spurt of pleasure warmed me, especially since I'd subconsciously hoped to run into him. His hands came to rest on my waist, big hands that practically burned my bared skin with awareness. His groin, flush with my ass, thrust and rubbed against me in a decadent dance. I leaned back into him, lifting my arms to drape around his neck. This gave him access to my neck, and he took advantage, his lips blazing a trail and sending an electric jolt right to my sex.

As we kept moving and grinding in time to the rhythm, I found myself not wanting the song to end. Could I stay in this electric moment forever, my desire flaming higher and higher as we moved in time? Every part of me quivered in anticipation.

His lips slid from my neck to the shell of my ear. "Baby, do you know how good you smell? I want to taste you. Lap your juicy little pussy until you come in my mouth."

Oh fuck. I almost melted into a puddle on the floor. I turned around and plastered myself to his front. Ignoring the tempo of the music and the crowd around us, he slowed our dance, even as my pulse raced faster.

I threaded my fingers into his silky hair and tugged him down to trace the lobe of his ear. I whispered, "After you lick me, I want you to fuck me, *hard*."

I didn't so much hear his groan as feel it, his whole body shuddering in reaction to my words. His firm hands slid from my waist to my full bottom, and he cupped my cheeks, molding me firmly against him. And I mean firmly. His erection pressed against me, so evident and tempting even through the fabric separating us. My pussy answered its call by soaking even further. If this kept up, I'd have a puddle under my feet.

Deciding we needed a little more privacy—because cops frowned on public sex acts, the prudes—I slipped out of his grasp. I gave him a come-hither look, one he quickly understood, and tugged him by the hand. Instead of following, he took the lead, his broad presence ahead of me making the club patrons scatter. I enjoyed the novelty of not having to push and shove my way out, just another reason a minion would be useful, especially a hot one like Drake, who I could think of so many uses for.

We emerged into the cooler night air, and instead of being pulled along, I found myself tucked into Drake's side, his warm, heavy arm draped around me, pressing me tight against his side.

"Where are you taking me?" I queried.

"Close by," he growled.

He wasn't kidding. We'd gone only a block when he pulled me into a dark alleyway and pressed me up against the brick siding of a building. Scorching lips found mine in a passionate kiss, a mashing of mouths and breath that shot tingles from the top of my head right down to my toes. I opened my mouth, and his hot tongue teased mine, the wet, sensual touch making my channel tremble pleasurably.

His hands caressed the bare skin of my waist, and I silently willed them to move south. Like a mind reader, he skimmed lower and tugged up the loose fabric of my mini skirt. Since I wore a G-string, his hands immediately made contact with the skin of my full ass, and he groaned against my mouth.

"You are so fucking hot."

I loved it when a guy talked dirty to me, but right now, I wanted action. "Shut up and touch me."

With a chuckle against my mouth, his hands got busy. One slid between my thighs and rubbed against the wet crotch of my panties. I dug my fingers into his shoulders. I needed to because my legs had turned to mush.

Drake continued to stroke me through the fabric of my undies, and I mewled and squirmed, so hot and horny I knew it wouldn't take much to send me over the edge.

"Tell me what you want," he growled in my ear before biting the lobe.

I didn't reply, just slid a hand between our bodies and squeezed his hard package. His rumbling groan accompanied his hips thrusting into my cupping hand.

"Fuck me," I whispered.

At my words, I felt his hands on either side of my hips and heard a tearing sound, followed by fresh night air on my lower lips, which signaled the demise of my panties. Offending material disposed of, his hands came back to cup my bottom, and he lifted me, pressing my molten core against his still hidden cock. The rough material of his jeans as he rubbed me against him made me throw my head back and moan loudly.

Even lost in the throes of passion, I couldn't miss the distinctive smell of brimstone.

"Demon!" I hissed. Drake immediately set me down, my skirt fluttering down to cover my bare crotch. I opened my eyes to scan the alley. I would have seen a lot more if Drake hadn't placed himself protectively in front of me. Totally macho, so totally hot. But I was a modern girl who didn't need saving from a man, and besides, I really wanted to kill whoever had interrupted what had been shaping up to be my greatest orgasm ever.

I slipped around to Drake's side and looked at the demons who'd come to pay a visit. Red-skinned with long, curving horns, these beasts were one of the nastier castes from Hell.

The biggest of them took a step forward and spoke. "Leave, shifter, our business is with the girl."

Drake's a shifter? I stored this interesting tidbit for later. Apparently, I had a date with some thugs. Before I could say a word, though, Drake spoke for me, with his fist.

The lead demon flew back and hit the opposite wall with a loud crash. He slid down the dented wall and slumped to the ground. For a moment, I wondered just what Drake's animal was because it took a lot of bloody strength to knock out a demon.

"Who's next?" asked my hero, um, I meant my wannabe minion.

Four more demons stepped forward, and I admit, I was impressed. Five demons to handle little ol' me? Ha, they'd obviously never watched me train. My dad had made sure at an early age I knew how to defend myself. He said a girl should be able to back up a "no" in case it wasn't heard

The irony never failed to amuse me because my dad, the demon of lust, ended up being an overprotective father. He claimed it was because he knew what males were thinking and no way were they doing those dirty things to his little girl.

But back to the fight. Drake charged the demons, and I would have applauded his balls—*I bet they're huge*—but I had my hands full with the two demons who decided to leap into the air and avoid Drake's mad dash. In a flash, I'd palmed my silver daggers, enchanted ones of course. Nothing but the best for Daddy's girl.

The thugs tried to flank me, but I kept the wall to my back, and when they dove on me, I sprang up then down, one high-heeled foot kicking out to one side while I slashed toward the other side with my blades. I connected in both instances and was rewarded with grunts of pain.

However, it wasn't enough to make them back off. The next few minutes were a blur as I dodged, feinted, and stabbed, the exhilaration of the fight making me laugh.

"Come on, you pussies," I taunted. Enraged, they charged me.

A slice through a hamstring here, a stab that nicked an artery there, a well-aimed kick at a pair of sensitive demon balls, and suddenly I found myself whirling to see my attackers disappearing through a portal back to Hell.

"Come back," I yelled at them. "I wasn't done with you yet."

A deep chuckle accompanied by clapping made me turn to see a deliciously rumpled and sweaty Drake. I gave him a mock bow.

"I have to give you credit," he said, shaking his head ruefully. "You really can take care of yourself."

"Thank you," I replied primly. My insides quivered in pleasure, though. I liked compliments as much as the next girl.

"Let's get you home before they come back with friends." I followed him out of the alleyway and watched as he hailed a cab. When it arrived, he opened the door and handed me in then closed it. I quickly cranked the window down and frowned at him.

"Aren't you coming with me?" Translation: *"Aren't you coming home with me so I can fuck your brains out?"*

He answered me with a hard kiss. My toes curled,

and my pussy started to throb. He broke off the heated embrace, his eyes glowing. "I'll see you tomorrow."

Then he tapped on the taxi's roof and stepped back. I refused to turn around and look at him with the stupid look females always have in movies. And the tears in my eyes weren't frustration; they were rage. *How dare he leave me horny, again!*

CHAPTER NINE

He watched the taillights of the taxi until they winked out of sight. A part of him wanted to follow, yet he knew, in his current state of mind, that wasn't wise.

"Bloody fucking hell!" Drake's anger coursed through him and needed an outlet. His fist hit the brick wall where, just moments ago, he'd almost taken Sally. However, the pain didn't clear up the white-hot rage still enveloping him at the knowledge the demons they'd fought wanted to hurt her.

How dare they! His beast roared and screamed in his head. Violent thoughts raced through his mind's eye as his animal came up with ways to punish the perpetrators—nasty, bloody, *permanent* ways. Revenge was why he'd sent her away, even as every ounce of his being had screamed for him to go with her. To claim her and place his mating mark upon her body, a warning to those who thought to hurt her.

But he wouldn't force his brand upon her until she agreed to it, possessive as both he and his beast felt. Life with his feisty intended would be a lot easier if she thought she had a choice.

However, while he worked on gaining her trust and affection—and invested in a jock strap, for she hadn't seemed happy he'd sent her away—he could use his skills and call in a few more favors to discover who dared try and hurt *his* woman.

And when I find them, I shall let them meet the wrath of my beast.

Crunch.

CHAPTER TEN

The cab ride home didn't take long, so as a result, I still simmered—and sizzled—my irritation equal to my arousal. And it was all HIS fault.

I didn't understand him. One moment he blew hot. Hot enough I wanted to blow him. The next, he sent me off, panties wet, lips swollen, and ready to scream.

It had to be a plot, one designed to drive me insane. There was only one solution.

Ride him like a cowgirl.

No!

Kill him.

Possibly. But I was thinking more along the lines it was time I avoided Mr. Too-Hot-And-Sexy. Reject me once, he was playing hard to get. Reject me twice, and that was it. Time to find myself another object of lust.

The ride, though, was just long enough for me to

make this decision, yet for some reason, I wasn't happy with it. Thus, I entered the apartment with a scowl.

As usual, Jezzie ignored my foul mood with a chirpy, "About time you got home." Apparently, someone had gotten into the sugar again because Jezzie bounced on the couch like a bunny on chocolate crack at Easter. She held the remote in one hand and pointed excitedly at the television screen.

Who cared what was on the news? I was more interested in the bag of chips on the table—regular rippled with a container of herb and garlic dip beside it. I consoled myself with lots of double dipping before I could finally focus on Jezzie, who stopped jumping and regarded me with a hand on her hip.

"Bad night?"

"Don't ask," I mumbled through a mouthful of chips.

"I don't need to ask, and you don't need to tell because I saw it all," she said with a wide smirk. She stepped aside and played the paused show in progress —you had to love DVR. It wasn't just any show on the screen. It was my reality show, featuring yours truly.

"Holy fuck." Like an idiot, I'd completely forgotten about the cameras following me, and they hadn't missed a thing from my hot dancing with Drake to our impromptu makeout session—I really liked the part where he ripped my panties off—to the foiled demon attack. It ended with the cab speeding away, but with a scene I hadn't seen—Drake cursing then turning to hit the brick wall behind him with a closed fist.

If he didn't want me to go, then why didn't he come with me? What suddenly had become more important than pleasuring my pussy and, in the doing, himself?

I would have liked to ponder it further, but an exuberant Jezzie wanted to know all the pertinent details.

"Is he a good kisser?"

"The best." I sighed. Suddenly, though, I found myself tired. I didn't want to think about what I'd almost experienced. For the first time in my life, my emotions were a muddled mess, and I didn't like it one bit. Something about Drake drew me like no other man ever before. I couldn't stop thinking about him and wanting him. It made no sense. I'd desired guys before, and no, I hadn't slept with all of them. I never used to have a problem walking away. But it was different with Drake. Why?

Sexual frustration. That had to be the answer. I refused to contemplate anything else. And it definitely wasn't the dreaded L word.

Ugh. Never. Love was for pussies. Love was for other people who didn't mind weakness. I wasn't weak.

A good shag was all I needed. Once I'd fucked him, say a dozen times or so, these weird feelings would disappear. I hoped.

The next day, I found myself back in the coliseum with a screaming crowd. Standing in the wings dressed in a strapless black bathing suit with painted flames licking up under my boobs from my crotch and black come-fuck-me boots—a totally bitching outfit—I peeked around the curtain and spotted signs in the stands. I leaned over to question Jezzie about them.

"Superhero names," she stated. "We've got it down to about a dozen now, and the voting has started."

"What are the top three so far?"

Feet shuffled nervously, and Jezzie preferred to stare at them instead of me. "Nothing's concrete yet," she said, hedging.

"Tell me." I crossed my arms and tapped my foot.

Jezzie sighed. "Just don't hurt me, okay? I didn't choose them. They're audience voted."

"You're stalling."

"One is Hell's Babe."

Not bad, kind of sexy actually.

"Bitch Slap."

Not too bad still, even if it made me sound more like trailer trash.

"Soul Slut."

"What?" I screeched, and she winced.

"Don't worry too much about that one. It's in third."

"It shouldn't have even made the list," I grumbled. I would have liked to argue about it more, but it was time for me to go stand in the spotlight as round two in the minion selection process began.

Seated on my throne, I listened to the announcer as he detailed the next task.

"A sidekick requires cunning. The ability to retrieve information and objects with none the wiser. Who of these five remaining contestants has what it takes to move on to the next round?"

Who indeed, I thought, tapping my fingernails impatiently on the armrest. The curtain hung in front of me, a heavy fabric shield that prevented me from seeing Drake, the jerk who'd left me hot and yearning the night before.

No more.

I'd spent too much time since last night thinking of him. Even though we'd met only two days ago, I was tired of him making me hot and heavy and not following through. Turn my legs to mush and not finish me off? Never again. I'd had it with him. Right after today's episode, I was going on a male hunt. I didn't care who I fucked at this point. I just needed someone with a dick who knew what to do with a horny woman. Drake wasn't the only guy who could turn my libido on. And I would prove to myself he was just another guy, nothing special about him.

I suddenly tuned back into what the announcer said. "The task was simple. Bring back an item without her realizing you'd taken it. A personal item that was recently in contact with her oh-so-luscious self."

Wait a second. *Are they talking about me?* Like fuck would I be giving anybody anything that dangerous. Items of a personal nature could be used in nefarious spells, something I liked to avoid. The curtain rose while I still wore a scowl from this latest turns of events.

I quickly smoothed my face into a smile, but inside, I seethed.

My five contestants stood in a row before me on a mini stage in the center of the coliseum. My eyes focused on one man only, though, and I found him watching me back just as intently. He raised a brow and gave me a sensual smile that sent a gushing heat to my pussy. Ugh. The jerk with his super-panty-creaming smile. I really needed to get laid.

My nails kept tapping as the announcer did his thing in his deep voice.

"First up, Dretnor. This savage demon comes from the outer rings and is the seventh son of a seventh son. He likes walks on the beach, a good grog of ale, and eviscerating his enemy. Tell us, Dretnor, what item from our lady Sally did you acquire?"

The tall demon bared his teeth in a toothy smile and strutted forward, holding forth a lock of hair.

It couldn't be mine. I would never give away a single tress.

The large, four-sided video screen hanging above the stadium lit up, and a video of me in the club the previous night dancing appeared. I watched as the demon in human guise cozied up to my backside and managed to snip off some hair unbeknownst to me as I gyrated, eyes closed.

The bastard had cut my hair. I seethed on the throne as I plotted his demise.

The crowd clapped, and I made a mental vow, after I'd ripped his intestines from his body, to always have my hair tied up tight when I went out partying in the future. The clip on the screen kept playing after Dretnor's impromptu trim, and the audience tittered when Drake appeared behind his boogying body and removed him, none too gently, to take his place.

I bit back a smile and quashed the warmth spreading through me. So what if Drake had shown jealousy? It changed nothing. He needed to learn he couldn't jerk me around. Maybe to irritate Drake, I'd shag Dretnor.

The emcee spoke. "Dretnor moves on. Next up, Allsor. This overgrown reptile hails from the wild swamps outside the ninth circle. In his spare time, he likes to bowl with skulls, play the banjo, and deep-fried, battered hellfrogs. Show us, Allsor, what you retrieved."

The lizard dude strutted forward and held out an envelope. The video screen lit up and showed him breaking into my postal box and stealing the piece of mail.

What a cop-out. I wasn't the only one to think so.

The crowd booed, and the announcer came back on. "We said something personal, pea brain. While the mail was addressed to her, she never touched your item. You have...failed!"

At his words, the folks in the stands cheered and then screamed in delight as a trap door suddenly appeared beneath lizard man's feet. With a gargling noise of surprise, down he went, disappearing from sight. I wondered if he'd be landing in the traditional alligator pit and thought it a pity they didn't show us. I'd have liked to have seen the outcome of that match.

Up next, the dwarf Raxnor, who had gone dumpster diving and found an apple core I'd discarded. Gross, but it fit the bill of the task.

Second last was the wolfman, named a boring Pete. He'd used his agility to sneak into my apartment and steal some eye shadow. Only one problem, it was Jezzie's, not mine. Like I would be caught dead wearing that shade of blue with my coloring, the idiot. Bye-bye, wolfman. Then it was the turn of the last contestant, the one who refused to get out of my mind: Drake.

I almost held my breath when he came forward, and my hands clutched at the armrests of the chair wetly. Surely I wasn't nervous for him? I wanted nothing to do with him and, by extension, didn't want him to win. Right?

With a cocky smile aimed right at me, even if my crotch bore the brunt, he whipped a scrap of fabric out of his pocket. I swear it was only the fact that cameras watched my every move and the approving roar of the crowd that kept me from diving on him and tearing the smile off his face. For dangling from his fingertips were the panties he'd ripped off me the night before.

I didn't remember the rest of the show—a foggy rage clouded my mind—but as soon as the curtain came down, I stalked off, grumbling darkly.

It took a bit of lube and some help from the backstage staff to peel the skintight bathing suit from me, and then more staff to help me yank on even tighter pants. I opted to wear a bra under my shirt—a shirt that wasn't even see-through. Gasp. I know, so conservative of me considering most of my outfits were designed to make me look like a high priced hooker. Those ladies of the night knew how to turn heads and get paid for it.

As I prepared to open a portal to head back to my place, a pair of strong arms wrapped around me from behind. Instinct kicked in, and my foot slammed down on my accoster's instep while, in the same motion, I jabbed back hard with my elbow.

I heard a grunt then a familiar voice whispered, "Is this foreplay?"

Drake. I should have known. "Let me go," I muttered through gritted teeth.

He didn't quite obey, loosening his arms only enough for me to turn in them to face him. When we were eye to eye, he tightened his arms again, pressing me against his hard length. I tried not to let the evidence of his happiness to see me, throbbing against my lower tummy, distract me. It didn't stop me from creaming myself, though.

He inhaled and smiled. "Your body seems happy to see me, but your face is saying a different thing."

"You asshole. I can't believe you made out with me just so you could steal my panties and move on to the next round."

He laughed, a throaty sound, which sent shivers down my spine. "Actually, I already had an item, an earring from our first encounter. What happened last night was because I want you, baby."

"Yeah, like I believe that after the way you left me hanging." I barely controlled my lips from curling into a pout, but my words still sounded petulant.

"It wasn't because I wanted to."

"Didn't look that way to me."

"I had urgent business to attend to."

In my world, nothing was more important than my needs. "Well, I have urgent *business* to attend to myself tonight, so if you don't mind..." I arched a brow and waited for him to let go of me.

He didn't, of course. Instead, he brushed his lips across mine, a move that made my breath hitch.

"I'm all yours tonight," he whispered. "Let me make it up to you."

"No, you had your chance." My mouth said one thing, but my body melting against him said another. Annoyed at my unwilling chemical reaction to his closeness, I decided to put a stop to his wooing attempt.

"I've already got plans to meet..." My mind worked furiously. "Dretnor. Yeah, demon boy really turned me on, too, last night, and I know he won't let me down."

Drake's eyes darkened, and his brows drew together in fury. I wondered if I was about to meet his beast—what fun.

Through clenched teeth, he growled, "You will not meet with that slug. If you have needs, I will take care of them. Know, right now, I will not allow another to touch you."

Talk about fucking possessive. My independent side cackled and prepared snide comebacks at his manly claim over my body. My feminine side just went incoherent with arousal. "We're not a couple. I'll see whoever I damned well please."

"Then I will kill them," he stated matter-of-factly.

Even my feminist side shut up at those words. Totally fucking hot—like caveman, retro hot.

"I don't get you," I grumbled. "Is this about winning? Do you think if you fuck me, you'll get an edge? I don't cheat," I stated—much. "Besides, anyone can tell you're not sidekick material. Why are you trying so hard?"

His face turned serious, and his eyes glowed as he replied. "Now that I've met you, I don't intend to let any other male come near you, sidekick or not. So if I need to win this competition to ensure you're one hundred percent mine, then I will do what I have to so I can win and have you to myself."

Hot damn. As speeches went, his was a definite panty dropper and shocker. It also smashed through my remaining resistance. "You'd do anything?" I whispered, leaning into him, mesmerized not only by the smoky look in his eyes but also his possessive words.

"Hell yeah, baby. Like I said, I'll kill if I have to. I don't share with others." With his spine-tingling declaration, my legs turned to Jell-O as he leaned down to kiss me.

This time, I wasn't letting him escape. Breaking off the embrace for just a moment, I opened a portal back to my bedroom and toppled us into it to land on my fluffy mattress.

He chuckled underneath me. "You don't waste time, do you?"

"I'm tired of waiting," I grumbled, my hands tearing at his shirt. I found it offensive. In a blink of an eye, he flipped us so I lay on the bottom and he straddled my waist. Grabbing the hem of his shirt, he pulled it off, revealing his perfect chest with his ripples of mouth-watering muscles. I reached up to touch his smooth skin, dragging my nails lightly down from his pecs to the waistband of his jeans.

He sucked in a breath, and I looked up at him. Glowing eyes met mine. "Your turn," he said huskily, and a moment later, I found both my shirt and bra removed and tossed to the side.

My nipples puckered under his scorching gaze. Slowly, he lowered his face and brushed it across my erect nubs. I sighed and arched, willing him to suck them. The hot flick of his tongue, circling around, forced a moan from me. I weaved my fingers through his hair and tried to force his mouth to take my engorged nipple into his mouth. He chuckled, his warm breath making them tighten even more.

"Oh no, baby. It seems like I've waited an eternity to touch you, and I intend to savor every moment." Suddenly, I found my hands removed from his hair, caught in an iron grip, and pushed above my head. I struggled to free my hands, but he held me firmly and continued his lazy exploration of my breasts.

My whole body thrummed like a live wire, anticipation stringing me taut. When he finally took my nipple into his mouth, I cried out and arched. It seemed as if he tortured me forever, his wet mouth sucking and pulling at my erect aureoles. He lavished attention equally between them, driving me senseless. Eventually, I gave up begging him to move lower, too lost in the erotic sensations he invoked. Besides, even though we were both clothed below the waist, it didn't stop him from settling between my legs and grinding his erection against my sex. My legs wrapped around his waist, cinching him tight.

When he finally stopped his torturous onslaught, my pussy had migrated past the point of wetness into flood territory. I ached for him and whimpered when his welcome weight left mine. I opened heavy eyelids to see him stripping down, and I also answered a few of my own questions. No, he didn't wear underwear, and hot damn, he was huge. Jutting proudly from his body, his cock bobbed at my perusal, and a glistening drop appeared. I licked my lips and went to sit up so I could lean forward and touch him. He pushed me back.

"Stay where you are." Under my hungry, disbelieving eyes, he gave me a wicked smile and grabbed his prick, his thumb smoothing his clear liquid over the swollen head. I almost came it was that fucking hot.

As if Drake sensed my rapidly dwindling control, his deft hands removed my skintight pants, and he grinned appreciatively when he pulled down my soaking panties.

He ran a finger down my moist cleft, and I shuddered. "Hands above your head holding the headboard," he ordered.

"What if I don't want to?" He was killing me slowly with pleasurable anticipation, and I needed to hurry things along so I didn't die before the main event. I spread my legs wide and bent my knees, exposing my Brazilian shave to him. There wasn't a male alive who could resist a shaved pussy, especially when I reached down to touch it. I stroked my finger over my velvety folds, wetting them, and then I drew my digit back to my mouth and licked it.

Eyes glowing, Drake crawled between my legs, intent and dangerous. My breath hitched. Face hovering over my sex, he blew on me hotly, and I gasped. "If you want me to devour that gorgeous pussy of yours, then grab that headboard and do not let go."

Fast as lightning, I grabbed the slatted wood. I still didn't understand why, when he ordered, I listened and, even more baffling, why it ramped up my desire.

His wide hands cupped my bottom and lifted me just enough to align my sex with his mouth. Thank Satan's horns, he didn't make me wait or beg. He instantly latched his mouth onto my sex, and at the first wet stroke of his tongue, I moaned. Then, like he'd done already with my poor nipples, he tortured me orally. He started with small flicks of his tongue against my clit, followed by his tongue probing between my lips. Then back to my clit, where he'd pinch it with his lips. Oh, the sweet fucking bliss. My fingers clutching the headboard were white-knuckled, and though I tried to arch, his hands held me firmly. I whimpered with need.

"Please."

He responded by letting go of my ass cheeks, but only so he could throw a heavy arm across my lower tummy while he used his other hand to stroke my slick folds. One finger penetrated me. Long and seeking, it found my G-spot and pressed on it. I let out a cry, and my body went taut.

"Don't you come yet, baby," he said in a gravelly voice. I opened my eyes to gaze down at him blearily. "I'm not done with you."

Then he inserted a second and third finger. He

could order me all he wanted, but when his tongue rapidly flicked my clit while his fingers pumped in and out of me, hitting and stroking my G-spot each time, it was a lost cause. My channel tightened almost painfully before spasming in orgasm. And still he finger fucked and licked me.

I keened, my pussy contracting hard, wave after wave of ecstasy roaring through my body. Just when I thought I'd black out from pleasure, he finally stopped his torture.

Lucky me, he wasn't done yet. The swollen head of his cock rubbed against my moist core, teasing me. I whimpered. It felt as if I hadn't just cum most wondrously. I wanted him so badly. I needed him inside me, pounding. I went to let go of the headboard to clutch him, but as if he read my mind, he growled.

"Don't you dare."

Another time, I'd find out what would happen if I disobeyed, but right at that moment, I didn't want to do anything that would stop me from savoring the delicious length of his cock, a treat he fed slowly into my aching sex.

I clenched the walls of my channel tightly around him, gratified to hear him grunt. It seemed to take forever before he'd seated himself fully in me, and once sheathed, he paused.

"Are you okay?"

I opened my eyes in disbelief, wondering if he was joking. But when I looked at him, he was quite serious, and I wondered if his cock size had caused him problems in the past. He certainly was well endowed, and it would explain his zealousness in prepping me. However, I really enjoyed the way he stretched me.

"The only way I won't be okay is if you don't stop pussyfooting and start fucking me."

Order or not, my hands came off the headboard and grabbed his ass just as I tilted my hips up. This had the effect of pushing him in a little deeper, fantastically so. And just to make sure he truly understood how much I liked the feel of him inside me, I squeezed him tightly with my sex and wrapped my legs around his waist, locking him in.

I almost made his eyes roll back in his head, and he got the point. His pelvis began to move, sliding his shaft in and out, his tempo increasing in pace with my cries. Yet, I still felt he was holding back.

"Harder," I panted.

He obliged, pistoning into me forcefully, his rapid-fire strokes building my pleasure. I tightened my hold on him, my breath whooshing in and out as I met him thrust for thrust. He grunted, and sweat beaded on his brow.

"Harder."

He didn't reply, but his jabs got more forceful. I no longer had the breath to speak or even moan, but our lovemaking was anything but quiet. I would almost dare say it was musical, a primal rhythm comprised of heavy breathing and the satisfying slap of flesh on flesh. As we moved together in time to the beat we created, my rapture built one pleasure block at a time until, like an unsteady tower, one little push sent it over. I found my voice again and screamed as I orgasmed once more, wave after wave of bliss quivering through me and leaving me shaking. Above me, Drake went still, and I opened my eyes to see him staring at me, his eyes completely black and glowing.

"Mine," he growled, and then he spurted inside me hotly.

Thank Satan's scientists for inventing the birth control pill. Between that and the fact that demons, even half ones, didn't get diseases, it made sex so much better without an icky layer of latex to ruin the moment.

Drake collapsed on me heavily, and I wondered when they autopsied me if they'd at least be able to tell I died happy. But a moment later, clutching me, he rolled until he lay on his back with me on top of him.

I looked down at him and grinned. "Thanks."

"Glad to oblige," he replied dryly.

The fire in my body temporarily extinguished, I found myself tongue-tied, an unusual state for me. Drake, thankfully, filled in the silence.

"What's your favorite color?"

I frowned at him. "We have amazing sex and you ask me something stupid like that?"

"I know you enjoyed yourself. You know I enjoyed

myself. Now I want to know more about the woman I'm going to fuck all night long."

Funny how, with those mere words, I could feel my pussy clench with an aftershock of pleasure. "Orange."

He snorted. "Seriously? I took you more for a pink kind of girl."

What could I say? I was full of surprises. "Let me guess, yours is black."

A mischievous smile tilted his lips. "Actually, it's pink." He punctuated his surprising remark by sliding the hand he had resting on my ass between my legs to rub against my sex. "This exact shade," he added as he tweaked my plump lips.

Ooh, I was definitely liking this conversation more and more.

His lips caught mine in a searing kiss, and he nibbled for a while before asking his next question. "What's your favorite movie?"

"The one we just made, baby," I replied, snickering when he pulled back with a wide-eyed look.

"You taped us?"

"No." I sighed regretfully. "But that doesn't mean it's not playing in my head."

He grinned widely, and I noticed the faint indent of a dimple in his cheek. He was so goddamned cute. And horny.

Lying on top of him, I couldn't miss the poking of his shaft as it rose and bumped against my backside. I loved that he had the stamina to match my libido because I was raring to go again. He'd teased me too many times for me to be satisfied with one quick bout.

But first, a little torture. I wiggled my ass against his jutting prick, but when he went to grab my hips, I shook my head. "I don't think so. Hands over your head."

With a smoky look that promised retribution—I couldn't wait—he laced his hands under his head. I then set out to explore the massive expanse of skin and muscle at my disposal.

My hands traced the powerful lines of his shoulders and arms. Even without his shifter blood, his physique would have ensured his strength. I couldn't wait to engage him in a wrestling match later. But for now, I was on an exploratory mission. I ran my hands lightly over his chest, stroking his flat nipples. A shiver went through him, and I arched a brow. Someone had a sensitive spot. Perfect, I'd found the first area of his body to exploit.

I leaned forward and blew on his nipple, already tight; nevertheless, it puckered further, and again, I felt a tremor. Gently, I took his nub between my teeth and applied pressure. He bucked, and a hand came loose to grasp my hair.

I looked up and met his darkening eyes, my lips curving mischievously. "Bad boy. Put that hand back."

His face taut and his eyes now glowing, he obeyed, but I could tell it killed him to listen—but hot damn, it made me horny. His cock jerked around behind me, especially when I leaned down and bit him again. But this time, though he shook and groaned, he let me have my way, and I tortured him. Unlike him, though, I couldn't keep it up for long because my own desire roared through my body, demanding satisfaction.

I pushed up from his chest and straddled him. "Tell me what you want," I said huskily.

"Ride me, baby."

My sex moistened, and I lifted myself until the tip of his cock nudged my cleft.

"That's it," he coaxed. "Sit that pretty pussy of yours onto my cock and fuck me, baby. I want to watch you come on my cock."

With a moan, I sat down hard, impaling myself. I'd forgotten how endowed he was, and I cried out as he filled me in a rush, the swollen head of his cock banging inside me so deeply I swooned for a second. I rocked back and forth on him lightly for a moment, adjusting myself to his girth, and then I got down to business. I braced my hands on his chest and rode him.

Some girls, when they ride a man astride, like to lift themselves up and down. Personally, I think that's a lot of work and does more for the guy. Me, I preferred to slide back and forth across his groin, his cock never actually leaving my channel, but pushing deep. Even better was the friction this placed on my clit. My nails dug into his chest as I moved back and forth, the direct and intense stimulation bringing me quickly to the brink and completely distracting.

I mewled.

"Want some help?" he growled.

I opened my eyes and had trouble focusing on him. Instead of answering, I just nodded. In a millisecond, he'd grabbed my hips and taken over for me, sliding me to and fro, sending my already throbbing clit into overdrive. My sex clenched at his cock tightly in a pre-orgasmic tightening.

"Fuck," he said with a groan, and then his cock pulsed inside me as he came. Like a signal, my channel contracted, and I collapsed on his chest as, once again, ecstasy rippled through my body in a never-ending wave that left me limp.

I felt his arms wrap around me, possessively, and his lips brushed the top of my head.

Then I did something I'd never done with any of my sexual partners. I fell asleep in his arms.

CHAPTER ELEVEN

When Drake awoke, the scent of sex hung heavy in Sally's bedroom, and he stretched with a grin.

What a night! In between bouts of lovemaking and power naps, they'd talked and talked. The more he'd learned about her, the more he wanted her. He'd refrained—barely—from marking her the previous night, something his beast was none too happy about. However, Drake had learned enough about Sally to know she wouldn't take kindly to him forcing the mating bond on her. Actually, she'd probably cut off his balls and feed them to him if he tried without her consent.

Given time—and lots of intense orgasms—he figured she would eventually choose him. Both he and his beast couldn't wait. In the meantime, though, he looked forward to enticing her to become his.

Speaking of whom, she lay draped over him like

the most decadent of blankets. He stroked her bare shoulder, and she shifted just enough on top of him to get his cock twitching. Her sleepy eyes opened, and she gave him a soft smile, which, framed by her wildly tangled hair, sent his erection from semi-hard to hang-a-flag in seconds.

"Mmm, I see someone's wide awake," she said huskily. She traced a path down his chest with her fingers right down to his cock. Wrapping her digits around him, she stroked him.

He arched into her touch, their lovemaking of the previous night not enough to sate him. Actually, a lifetime of loving her would probably never be enough.

He removed her hand from his prick, and she looked at him, puzzled. "Hold that thought," he told her. He rolled off the bed and stood. She smiled at him wickedly and slid her hands down over her belly to the mound between her legs. She parted her thighs and cupped herself.

Drake's cock jerked, straining toward the molten core she teased him with. But he wanted something specific this morning. He strode into her bathroom and prepped the shower. When he came back into the bedroom, one of her hands still stroked her pussy while the other rolled and pinched an erect nipple. She'd closed her eyes and pretended not to notice him. The little tease.

My tease...

Drake leaned over and bit her nipple. Squeaking,

she opened her eyes. Before she could protest, he scooped her up and carried her into the bathroom. He didn't let her go until he'd stepped into the shower. Once under the hot, cleansing spray, he released her, sliding her slowly down his body until she stood on her own.

"Trying to tell me something?" she said with a grin when he grabbed a bar of soap and set himself to the task of washing her.

Drake just leaned forward and kissed her, enjoying her "ooh" against his mouth when he slid his hand between her thighs and soaped her cleft.

Then he stepped back and soaped himself, ending with his turgid cock. Watching her with hooded eyes, he stroked himself, enjoying the way she licked her lips and her eyes followed his moves.

He moved toward her and pushed her back so he could rinse himself with the hot spray. He chuckled at the feel of her hands grasping his cock and tugging.

Moving back, he leaned against the cold tile wall and crossed his arms over his chest. "Get on your knees and suck me."

"Excuse me." Her hand on his cock stilled, and she looked at him, her expression torn between indignation and pleasure.

"Suck my cock," he whispered. To punctuate his order, he threaded his fingers through her wet hair and pushed her down. Her eyes glazed over, and she licked her lips as she dropped to her knees in the tub.

Eye level with his cock, she stuck out her tongue and licked the tip. Then, more boldly, she laved his shaft from head to base. But he wanted more from her. And with the hour growing late, he couldn't wait.

"Open your mouth, baby, and blow me."

With a strangled moan, she obeyed, her mouth opening wide and inhaling as much of his shaft as she could take without gagging. He let her get away with that for a few strokes in and out, her cheeks hollowing as she suctioned him hard. Then, on the fifth pump into her wet orifice, he thrust a little deeper. Her hands slapped against his thighs, and she dug her nails in. He groaned when her throat squeezed around him convulsively, but he held the position, and she relaxed, resuming her oral pleasure of his prick, but now taking him deeper.

Drake closed his eyes and let his head fall back, both he and his beast basking in the oral attention of the woman who would be their mate. When he felt his cock swell, ready to burst, he went to pull out. But his little hellcat had different plans. She clamped her lips tightly around him and one of her hands grasped his balls and squeezed.

"Fuck, baby, you're gonna make me come."

She moaned around the steel rod in her mouth, and when he looked down and saw her eyes looking at him, hot with desire, he lost control. Heavy cream spurted from him in molten jets, and his hot lady swallowed it all, sucking him dry. Shudders permeated his body as she drained him.

After what seemed like an eternity of bliss, she finally let his cock loose. But his excellent sense of smell could tell she was still highly aroused. Reversing their positions, in a flash he had her pressed against the wall, his hands holding her up, for her legs went limp the moment his mouth touched her sex.

Her desire coated her plump lips in a juice sweeter than ambrosia, and he feasted on it, his tongue alternately lapping inside her core and then flicking across her swollen nub. Her cries grew more and more frantic, their sound rousing his cock for another round. Still holding her around the waist, he stood and lifted her. The head of his cock nudged her cleft, and he hissed when she thought to take control again, wrapping her legs around his flanks and drawing his shaft in.

But now, locked in position, astride him, he controlled the pace. He pushed her back against the wall, and securing one arm around her waist, he leaned his torso away so his other hand could pinch and rub her clit. Her pussy squeezed around him at his touch, and he increased his pace, loving how she could take what he had to give and still beg for more.

Harder he pistoned his hips, her mewls of pleasure changing frequency as she neared her peak. Faster he thrust, the tight, clinging feel of her sex driving him wild.

And then she cried out his name as she came. "Drake!"

The sweetest sound he'd ever heard, followed by the most incredible sensation as her channel convulsed around his rod. With a roar his beast echoed in his mind, he came again, bellowing, "Mine!"

All mine.

CHAPTER TWELVE

As soon as Drake stepped through a portal to his apartment, I missed him and wondered when I'd get to see him again. Crazy as it was, I was falling for the guy.

Gasp.

No.

The shock of the revelation saw me sitting up in bed. Surely I was misinterpreting my emotions. But crazy as it was, and foreign as well, I—the love 'em and leave 'em gal—missed a man. Wanted a man. Not just any man, Drake.

"No, no, no." I rushed to look at myself in the mirror, and my familiar features stared back. Physically, I hadn't changed, but inside, oh damn it all to Hell, I cared for him.

How and when had it happened? Sure, I'd lusted after his body, and I'd admit he was the best lover I'd ever encountered. But this was all about sex. No emotions. Just great sex with some conversation and cuddling thrown in.

I groaned and dove on the bed, hiding my head under the pillow. How could this have happened? And an even better question, what would I do about it?

Drake had implied he'd be sticking around for a while, a thought that didn't send me in a panic and rushing for an airline for an impromptu vacation in a very remote location. Actually, I'd kind of gone all soft and warm inside when he'd promised to see me after the show.

Speaking of which, I had to get ready. Hopping out of bed, I had another shower since the first one had led to more sex and... Well, let's just say I had some sticky areas that really needed cleaning.

The titillating memories of the morning, the previous night, the middle of night, and the shower wouldn't stop running through my head so that, when I finally wandered out of my room, I couldn't help the silly grin plastered on my face.

"I see someone had a good night," Jezzie said with a wide smirk.

A beatific smile plastered to my lips, I poured my coffee and told her, "Drake slept over."

Liquid spewed as Jezzie choked on her java. "You did what? Is he still here?" she wheezed.

"No, he had to leave to get ready for the competition today."

Jezzie suddenly looked nervous, and I watched her suspiciously as she chattered brightly about inane topics while making breakfast and then tidying up. Given Jezzie never did either, it wasn't hard to figure out something was up.

"What are you hiding?"

"Me?" She opened her eyes wide in feigned innocence.

"Spill it before I tell about the Rocky Mountains incident on national television." I knew more than one secret she wanted to keep under wraps.

Sweating and fidgeting, she tried to avoid my eyes, but I possessed a pretty good glare when riled. It was only a matter of time before she caved and divulged. "It wasn't my idea, honest to Satan. But the network, they said it would make an awesome segment, and I didn't realize when we'd signed the contract, they'd included the clause to–"

Impatient, I interrupted. "What's going to happen today?"

"Each of the three remaining contestants has to discover and divulge a juicy secret about you or that directly relates to you. It might be something you know or don't."

My mind worked furiously. What secrets did I hide? A few, like any semi-demon of my age, mostly schoolgirl pranks I'd gotten away with. As for something involving me without my knowledge, well, I'd admit that was information I'd like to know, actually.

"It's okay." I said the words absently, suddenly wondering what secret Drake would reveal. The way I liked it when he bit down on my nipple as he fucked me? No, not secret enough, just ask any of my previous lovers. I both dreaded and anticipated what I'd learn, and in front of an audience.

Things kept hidden should remain so, for the simple reason revelations usually meant someone would get hurt—then killed. Demons, even half ones, weren't known to turn the other cheek. Vengeance was our middle name. Seriously, according to the public registers of Hades, Vengeance ranked number one for middle names followed by Misery.

I now wondered more than ever what Drake would do to win this round. What secret about me had he discovered? And would whatever he revealed force me to never see him again?

It wasn't just my mind that screamed "no!" to that scenario. My head and heart did, too.

I spent the day in a nervous state. Pacing. Eating. Eating some more. An ass like mine didn't happen overnight; it took work.

In an almost trance, I readied for my appearance on the reality show that I now regretted. I just wanted this farce over with. Wanted to return to my old life of collecting escaped souls, shaking my booty in clubs, and shopping. But my old life didn't have the hot and delicious Drake.

Argh.

The moment of truth, literally, arrived. I barely heard the emcee as he detailed the task for the remaining minion contenders. Okay, I lied. I listened to every word and alternated between simmering irritation and nervousness. I'd take battling a creature with claws and spitting acid over dread any day.

This time, when the curtain lifted, revealing me on my throne, I didn't smile. My eyes veered right over to Drake and held his gaze. His face didn't betray any emotion, something I didn't find reassuring.

First up stepped the dwarf, looking nervous for once. He fidgeted before the microphone, and I impatiently squirmed, too, not really giving a shit about what he had to say.

"The secret I discovered—um..." Raxnor trailed off and peered down at his feet encased in dirty work boots. He swallowed audibly. "Sally's middle name is Dawn, and her mother was a country singer."

I lost some of my tension and giggled. Okay, I'll admit the fact that the woman who'd birthed me liked to croon corny western songs embarrassed me and was a fact I assiduously hid, but really, it wasn't that big of a deal. And as for the stupid middle name, again, blame my momentarily insane father. Talk about boring revelations.

Apparently, the crowd agreed with me. They booed and jeered as the dwarf's already ruddy face turned an even brighter shade of red. At least he didn't cry out with fear when the trap door beneath his feet opened and he tumbled down. Rumor said the hidden chasm led to the home of the lamia—half-snake, half-women; those nasty bitches knew how to make a man scream, just not in actual pleasure.

The spectators cheered wildly. They did so love a loser.

I couldn't help myself. Over and over, my gaze strayed to Drake, a man who'd made me feel things I never expected. Things I wasn't sure I was ready for. I tapped my nails on the armrest on the throne, wondering what secret he would reveal, and to my chagrin, I worried it would change how I felt about him.

What went on behind his placid expression? As my glance went to him again, his eyes held mine, and I imagined he tried to convey something, but mind reading was my half-sister's ability, not mine. Whatever secret he planned to reveal, I'd have to wait a moment longer, for the demon Dretnor approached the microphone next.

I didn't like the nasty gleam in his eye, nor the bared teeth as he smirked. Why did I suddenly get the impression he wasn't truly on my side? Ridiculous. If he didn't want the job as my minion, why compete?

"My secret is one Sally the half-demon is unaware of and involves another contestant."

My stomach tightened into a knot, and fear made me sound harsh. "How am I supposed to know you're telling the truth and not spouting some load of garbage to try and discredit your opponent?"

"I submit myself and the secret I have to tell to the Fire of Truth."

The crowd oohed, and even I sucked in a surprised breath. To the ignorant, the Fire of Truth was a spell cast upon a being who wished to prove the veracity of their words. It surrounded the speaker in a nimbus of flames. If they told the truth, the flames didn't touch them. Lie, and they burned alive for the next millennium. Not exactly the most pleasant fate.

As denizens of Hell, truth wasn't something often seen or heard of. Hence, the spell was rarely seen. The fact that Dretnor offered to submit to it meant he believed the information he'd found was sound. I hoped so for his sake because the spell didn't care how much a being believed in what they said, or if they'd been misled. If the information imparted was false, they'd burn anyway.

Dretnor must have warned the show producers of his intention, for barely a moment passed before a cloaked figure stepped onto the dais with the demon below.

Raising his arms and chanting in a guttural tongue that made me shiver, the mage enchanted Dretnor. With a small whoosh, blue flames ignited on Dretnor's body. Again, the crowed oohed, and my stomach drew tighter.

The mage stepped away, and Dretnor moved to the

microphone, a triumphant leer on his dark demonic lips. Slowly, the crowd quieted and leaned forward in expectation, as did I.

"Drake is half-demon, half-shifter: dragonshifter." The crowed aahed, and I sat back stunned. I'd known Drake had shifter blood, but dragon, the rarest of all types, that surprised me. But it wasn't a big deal. Actually, it made him hotter. I wondered if he could fly. I also wondered why he hadn't told me. Surely he didn't think I'd kill him and skin him for his prized skin, tempting as the idea would be to some.

Drake's face tightened, and I suddenly knew this wasn't the only secret.

Dretnor smiled, his pointed teeth glistening. "He's also misrepresented himself to our prospective employer. The first night he met her, he was tasked with discrediting her or, even worse, allowing her to be killed. He also, after the demon attack outside the club, made inquiries into the bounty placed on her head and offered himself up as an assassin, should the patron of the first attempt wish to pay for a second."

I shook my head no, but the flames around Dretnor burned merrily without a sizzle or a pop. Sickening to say, I really wanted him to start screaming. I knew my heart was. And, by Satan's horns, did it hurt.

My tear-filled eyes—damned dust—met Drake's, and I read the truth in his eyes. "You bastard," I whispered, a word the invisible microphones picked up and echoed around the stunned audience in the coliseum.

Dretnor, pleased with himself, stepped back and crossed his arms. It was over. He'd won. The crowd went wild.

But wait... Drake strode to the microphone and held up his arms. It took a moment for the audience to notice, and when they did, the heavy silence hung with anticipation.

"Cast the spell of truth on me." A cacophony arose at Drake's words.

What was he doing? Even in my pain over his betrayal, a part of me didn't want to see him hurt, not until I'd had a chance at him, the rotten, lying jerk.

The mage stepped quickly onto the stage for the second time and cast the spell of truth. The blue flames sprung up around Drake, dancing along his tanned skin.

His eyes met mine, and I couldn't look away. "Yes, I am a dragonshifter. I didn't tell you because I wanted to get you used to me before I let you know of my beast. It is not easy for me to trust, knowing how my kind are hunted." The flames burned steadily, his words truthful. But we both knew his dragon wasn't the real issue.

My hands squeezed tightly around the armrests of the throne. "And when we met, were you there to discredit me?"

"Yes, I admit someone hired me to make you look bad or, if I had the chance, allow the soul we both hunted to kill you. And I'd planned to do it. I'm a mercenary and bounty hunter. Give me the right price and I will do just about anything. But once I saw you, I changed my mind. I couldn't hurt you." The flames didn't crisp him.

But that didn't absolve him. "You stole my bounty." And dammit, he'd stolen my heart.

"Aah, but that didn't actually hurt you, did it? However, it did get your attention right where I wanted it. On me."

"Were you hired to kill me?" I wondered if I should feel flattered he'd decided to fuck me before killing me. When did he plan to do it? The next time we got naked and I was vulnerable?

"I did make myself available should someone wish to put out a contract on your life."

One large tear rolled down my cheek, and a crushing pain enveloped me, not a physical one but mental, a debilitating sensation, one that made me drop my head and stifle sobs.

"But I never intended to actually kill you."

I waited for him to start screaming at his obvious lie. When not even a whimper sounded, I looked up and met his eyes filled with sorrow.

His eyes pled with mine. "The offer of my services as assassin was to flush out whoever wanted to hurt you so I could kill them and keep you safe. I would never harm you." The flames didn't even flicker.

Truth.

"Why not?" A simple question meant to convey a dozen questions I couldn't voice.

"The moment I met you, my beast recognized you as our mate."

I snorted. "Great, so because your dragon wants me, you decided to pursue me instead of killing me."

"My dragon wants you, very much, but the man, he wants you even more. You intrigue me, Sally. I love your feisty attitude. I love the way you kick ass. I love that thing you do with your tongue. Don't you get it? I love you."

Now I really expected him to start screaming as the Fire of Truth seared his lying skin from his body, but the flames still danced harmlessly.

Oh, by Satan's horns, he told the truth. I tried to get up and run away from the love in his eyes, from the love bursting forth from my heart. I couldn't give in to it. Love would hurt me, destroy me. Make me into someone I wasn't.

A force held me in place, though. I vaguely heard the crowd cheering and whistling. Then the emcee boomed. "Both have told a deep dark secret and proven their worth. There is only one challenge left now. Tune in tomorrow to see who will be the *Last Sidekick Standing*."

The curtain dropped, and the invisible force holding me let go and I ran, straight to the only person I trusted. The one who truly loved me. Daddy.

CHAPTER THIRTEEN

My father's reception room overflowed with females—demons, souls, and beings belonging to realms outside Earth and Hell. I pushed my way through them, looking for my father, who lounged amidst his harem.

Although he'd lived centuries, my father didn't look any older than a man in his mid-forties. By choice. He could choose whatever appearance he wanted, but he preferred that of a man who'd lived, a man with character.

I didn't care what he looked like. I only wanted the comfort my daddy could offer.

As soon as he spotted me, he clapped his hands and shooed his lovebirds away. As a demon of lust—some humans once upon a time had even worshipped him as a god—he was never without female company, and, sometimes, even males accompanied him. But I always came first.

I threw myself on my father, burrowing my face into his chest, and noisy sobs escaped me, such a rarity.

"Who do I need to kill?" he asked in a voice dripping with frost.

Daddy dearest always knew what to say to make me feel better. "Me, for being such an idiot."

"What is it, Sally-bird? What's happened?"

Um, was my father the only one in Hell not watching HBC and its ongoing saga, also known as my life, the unfolding disaster? "It's awful, Daddy."

"Is this about that Drake boy? Do I need to have him hung up by his toenails and have his entrails ripped out?"

"Yes." Then quickly before he sent out the order, "No. He said me loved me, Daddy."

"The bastard," said my father in a choked voice.

I peered up at him to see him stifling a grin. "You jerk. You knew why I was here."

Daddy laughed. "Of course I did, you idiot. You're my little girl. I know about everything that happens to you. So Drake admitted, under a spell of truth no less, he loves you. What's the problem?"

"I don't want love," I grumbled.

"Excuse me?"

I shouted. "I said I don't want love."

"Why ever not?" I couldn't believe the note of incredulity in his voice.

"Love is for pussies. It makes a person weak and do stupid things."

My father dumped me off his lap and stood up. "Listen here, young lady, I don't know where you got those foolish notions, but you need to readjust your thinking. Love, contrary to your belief, makes you stronger."

"I notice you don't deny it makes us do dumb shit though."

"No, I won't deny it. Love will make you do things you never would have dreamed of, but you want to know a secret?"

"What?"

"Those stupid things will make you insanely happy."

His answer made no sense. How could acting like an idiot make me happy? Then I thought of Drake and the laughter we'd shared the previous night and, to my disgust, I actually understood what my father was telling me. I really hated it when he was right. But it didn't mean I forgave Drake. The prick had lied to me. Maybe I would skin him and make boots out of his dragon hide.

As if thinking of him conjured him, he strode into the room. My father looked at Drake with his stony face then to me with my stubborn look. He sighed. "Good luck, son, you're going to need it."

Then my father left me with *him*. My eyes couldn't help drinking him in, from the partially unbuttoned shirt that strained over his bulging muscles, to his snug jeans, where evidence of his arousal distended them. I left his eyes for last because, once I gazed into them, I found myself caught as if in an emotional vortex.

"What are you doing here?" I tried to control the trembling of my voice.

"I've come to collect my mate."

"I'm nobody's mate. Go find yourself somebody else." Brave words considering just the thought of him with another woman made me want to growl.

"You are mine. I thought to give you time so that you would come to me of your own volition, but I see now it would have never happened. I don't know why you refuse to admit you love me."

"Maybe because I don't love you."

"Liar."

"I don't care what you think. Now go away."

"Not without you."

The steely glint in his eye gave me a moment's warning, and I whirled to flee. But he had no intention of letting me go, and while I'd never admit it aloud, I didn't want to escape.

But just because he'd caught me and proceeded to carry me back to his lair didn't mean I'd give in easily. Stubbornness was one of my most endearing qualities.

CHAPTER FOURTEEN

Drake could see the fear and confusion in her eyes, a look she'd worn since she'd heard the truth, both Dretnor's and his own. His dragon paced and railed inside his body, torn between lamenting his mate's distress and a desire to tear apart the demon who'd thought to separate them.

When she'd fled after the fiasco, he'd searched her out backstage, but she'd already escaped. He'd flashed to her apartment and found it empty. Desperate to find her and explain himself, he'd gone to her father's home in Hell next. Lo and behold, he'd found her, spitting mad. Probably not the right moment to tell her how sexy it made her.

Throwing her over his shoulder to take her back to his place seemed like a good idea at the time, but even with his excess strength, her wiggling body, not to mention well-aimed jabs at his kidneys, made him think he would have been better off tranquilizing her first.

Her violent assault was also punctuated by vile insults, some so original he made note of them for future use. A delicate shrinking violet she was not. Fuck, did he love her toughness.

With the use of a portal, he finally made it inside his place, a retrofitted cave in the bowels of a mountain situated within the Rockies. He liked his privacy. Setting her down, he moved back quickly as she whirled with flying fists.

"Rotten, scum-sucking bastard. I'm going to tear your intestines out and tie you up with them. I'm going to—"

"Tie you up and gag you if you don't simmer down and listen," he stated calmly. His cock, on the other hand, swelled; apparently, it hoped she'd keep up her histrionics.

Her eyes narrowed at him dangerously, but he caught the scent of her arousal, not to mention he couldn't miss seeing the way her nipples hardened into pebbles and protruded through her shirt.

Thank Satan, she liked a bit of kink. He was more than happy to oblige. Taking the brunt of her punches and kicks with not even a grunt escaping him, he wrapped his arms around her tightly and carried her screaming invectives into his bedroom. He tossed her onto the bed and dove on top of her, covering her squirming body with his own. She bucked under him deliciously, and he grinned at her, even as he bound her hands to the fur-lined manacles that hung from the top corners of his bed.

She finally shut up, and her eyes widened. Her sweet little tongue licked her lusciously full lips, and he held back a groan as he gripped her ankles to spread them. He manacled them as well and stood back to look at her, spread-eagle on his bed. Only one thing ruined the view. Pulling out a dagger, he straddled her suddenly still body.

She said not a word, but her eyes grew wide as saucers. Once again, though, she showed her mettle, not even flinching when he sliced through her clothing and pulled it away, leaving her naked.

"I hate you," she said finally when he stood back to admire her nude body.

"Your body says otherwise."

"Just because we're about to have awesome sex doesn't mean I've forgiven you," she stated.

He grinned and arched a brow. "Don't worry. I intend to make it better than awesome, and I'm not releasing you 'til you say the words I want to hear."

"How's fuck you?" she said with a nasty smile.

"Now, baby, is that any way to talk to your mate?" He shook his finger at her. "It's that kind of language that is going to earn you a spanking."

"You wouldn't dare!"

He just smiled and pulled a paddle out from the chest at the foot of his bed.

Again, her eyes widened, and then she turned into a hellcat. She thrashed and pulled at the restraints, and while her words screamed scorn and disgust, her pussy glistened and the smell of her lust permeated the air.

Time to make her scream...in pleasure.

CHAPTER FIFTEEN

Tied to his bed, exposed to his view, my day was looking up. I was still pissed at him, though, and I realized most of my anger didn't come from his deception but from his declaration that he loved me. Even worse, I could feel my own emotions leaning toward him, the words sitting on the tip of my tongue begging for release. And no matter what my father said, I didn't know if I was ready for that type of commitment. I'd rather take a dive off a really high cliff.

However, he had no qualms, and he crawled onto the bed between my legs, every inch of him vibrating with sensual energy, the black paddle gripped between his teeth. Warmth suffused me without volition. He ended up straddling my waist and stroking the flat edge of the paddle over the tip of my erect nipples.

"It's a shame I already bound you on your back,

else I would have enjoyed putting you over my lap and smacking that naughty bottom of yours."

I shuddered.

"Have you ever been spanked, Sally?"

I shook my head, unable to reply as he continued to drag the cold paddle across my breasts.

"I think you'd like me to punish you, Sally. I know I'd enjoy it. You, squirming on my lap, naked and begging. Maybe I wouldn't even use a paddle. I think I'd enjoy the skin-to-skin feel of my hand on your tender skin." He slapped my tit, not hard but enough to surprise a gasp from me. Even more liquid heat shot to my groin, and I had to bite back the urge to ask him to act out his words, the sensual imagery so arousing.

"You know what else I think you'd like?" he asked, sliding back so he straddled my thighs. "I have a flogger comprised of dozens of thin latex strands. Maybe I should take it out and whip your pussy instead, as punishment for trying to deny me." He brushed his knuckles over my mound, and my hips arched.

"Please," I finally begged, my whole body screaming for him to stop playing and touch me. I needed him to relieve some of the pleasurable pressure building inside me.

"So many things I want to do to you, Sally, but for now, I think I shall content myself with this." His thumb found my clit and rubbed while, at the same time, he leaned forward and caught my nipple between his lips. Instant bliss made me cry out and quiver. I couldn't deny I loved it when he touched me, every caress stoking my desire, higher and higher. He toyed with me, his mouth alternately sucking and biting my nubs as his hand worked my cleft, one moment tweaking my clit, the other sliding between my plump lips and finger fucking me.

I felt my pleasure building, a coiling tension in my body that needed just a little push to send me over the edge into pure bliss.

He stopped. Confused, I opened my bleary eyes. "Please," I moaned.

"Tell me."

"Fuck me," I replied, trying to arch my hips, but his hands on my thighs held me pinned.

"No, baby, tell me you love me. Tell me you're mine."

"No." I thrashed my head.

The moment I gave him the wrong answer, he attacked my body again with his tongue and mouth. And it felt so damned good.

This time, he put his mouth on my sex, sucking at the cream my arousal produced, his tongue probing my inner channel. When he shoved three fingers into my pussy while sucking on my clit, I almost came, the rapture so intense.

He pulled back again. "I love you, baby. Say the words. Just 'I love you,' and I'll fuck you like you need."

I thrashed my head no, even as my whole body

screamed yes. He chuckled, a low sound that made my tummy curl.

"Such a glutton for punishment. I think I will use my flogger after all."

I opened my eyes in shock and watched as he leaned over the side of the bed and reappeared holding a small flogger.

"Don't you dare," I gasped, my nipples tightening so hard they almost hurt.

"Say the words," he replied with a naughty glint in his eyes.

I tightened my lips.

He twirled his wrist, and the flogger struck me, right between the thighs against my mound. My flesh, already over sensitized, screamed in delight, as did I. Over and over he slapped my flesh with his torturous toy, the silken latex strands feathering and stinging lightly against my cleft, ramping up my desire higher and higher.

He stopped the flailing and plunged several fingers inside me. I screamed and trembled, tightening my muscles around them, about to come. He pulled them out again.

I whimpered. I couldn't take the pleasure anymore. I opened my mouth to say the words he longed to hear, the words I felt as much as I wanted to deny them, but I was saved—or damned—by the ringing of the phone.

With a sigh and a slap of his hand across my mound that made me shudder, he got off the bed and walked away. I hungrily watched the delicious view of his naked, taut buttocks as he left, but as my body cooled, I got annoyed. Like hello, naked, hot babe tied to the bed—make that a very horny babe. For a guy who claimed I was his mate and was trying to make me say the big L word, he had an odd sense of timing. They hadn't invented voicemail so you could leave a woman in a high state of sexual arousal to answer the phone.

My confusion grew even more when he reappeared, fully dressed.

"I've got to go out for a little bit."

What? "You're kidding, right?"

His rueful look didn't have a trace of humor. Neither did his hard kiss, which left me breathless.

"I'll be back as soon as I can," he murmured against my lips while his hand stroked across my damp folds.

He started to walk away. "Um, aren't you forgetting something?" I asked.

He turned to look at me and gave me a chagrined look. "Sorry." He walked back, but instead of releasing me, he grabbed a remote and flipped HBC on.

My mouth opened wide, and my eyes even wider as, with a grin and a blown kiss, he sauntered out of the bedroom. The bastard! I growled and thought of expending some of my special demon strength and breaking the bonds. I mean, seriously, tough as his chains might look, my special blood made me stronger.

But I knew he knew I could get free, and obviously, he expected something of me.

So I wondered, should I break free and check his place out? Break free and leave so he could chase me down again? Or did I stay as I was and wait for him to come back and continue where he'd left off? Too many choices and I didn't know which to choose, although I was starting to get a headache thinking about it.

With nothing better to do for the moment, and undecided still as to my best option, I watched HBC, and surprise, it was a rerun of the last episode of *Last Sidekick Standing*.

Watching the entire drama unfold was a little easier this time round, not to mention I saw some extra footage I hadn't noticed at the time. Such as Dretnor scowling as Drake passed his own test of truth. I still didn't get that demon. He didn't even seem to like me, so why did he care? When the curtain came down at the end of the episode, and the cameras showed my hasty departure, I expected the show to end at this point.

Instead, the emcee came on and announced that, due to exciting developments, the show's regular time slot had been extended. Curious at the fresh footage the emcee hinted at, I watched avidly as Dretnor hurried off, looking around him suspiciously as he scurried through Helltown and entered the offices of...HOE.

What the fuck was Dretnor doing there?

"It looks like there is more than one devious plot unfolding. Is Dretnor truly after the sidekick position, or has he joined the competition for nefarious reasons? Find out more after this commercial break brought to you by Hell-A-Roni, Hades' favorite supper treat."

My mind worked furiously as I tried to think of an ulterior motive for Dretnor. Was he after my soul hunting job? It made no sense, as anyone could apply for a soul hunter position. Of course, the mortality rate tended to make it almost impossible to get life insurance, but nothing prevented him from applying. I didn't think he had a secret sexual yen for me. We'd never even spoken, and while Drake's lust shone in his eyes whenever he saw me, Dretnor's reflected only dislike.

I really hoped Drake won the competition because I really couldn't see myself working with the demon. Not to mention, I knew I wouldn't last much longer under Drake's torturous method of getting me to confess my feelings. But damn was I enjoying myself while he tried.

The commercial break ended, and the emcee came back on, along with video footage of Dretnor opening a portal and stepping out into a mountain range.

"What is our villainous competitor doing outside his only opponent, Drake's, home? Is he planning to kill the only other contestant, or does he have more sinister plans?"

Outside Drake's home? Surely, I'd misunderstood.

I continued to watch the television and saw Dretnor blast a hole in the rock, and unless Drake had a really wicked television set, I actually felt the tremor in the bed.

The ominous music playing on the television kind of matched the oh-shit feeling creeping through my limbs. The camera switched, and I caught a brief glimpse of my naked flesh on the television screen, as suddenly my spread-eagle predicament was broadcast to the world.

Great. Just great. They were shooting this live, which meant I didn't have time to admire my curvy body. I needed to get free. Drawing on my demon side, I pulled at my restraints, my muscles screaming in protest. With a clang and sudden jingling, I freed one arm, albeit with a new heavy bracelet. With one arm free, I was able to use both hands to pull free my other bound arm.

I'd managed to snap one of the chains holding my legs when Dretnor appeared in the bedroom doorway.

"You weren't invited to this party," I told him, doing my best to shield my body with my hair. Some men I liked to pose for; others, I preferred to gouge their eyes than let them feast on the awesomeness known as Sally.

He didn't leave. Rather, he grinned at me, a nasty look full of sharp teeth that went quite well with his evil, glowing eyes. "If it isn't the slut herself," he said, approaching with heavy feet, just as I broke the last chain.

Slut? I totally resented that claim. There was nothing wrong with being sexually liberated—unless you were liberating with someone else's man.

Freed, I bound up on the bed, heavy chains flying. "What are you doing here?"

"Isn't it obvious? I'm here to kill you."

"Why?" I know, stupid question to ask when I should have been looking for ways to kick his ass, but I truly wanted to know. I mean, come on, I was standing buck naked in front of the guy, um, demon, and while every other male in the known planes would have been sporting a hard-on, he wanted to snuff me. Something was seriously wrong with this picture.

"Once you die, my beautiful Meddie will be mine."

"Who the fuck is Meddie?" Seriously, I had no idea, and why did he need to kill me to be with her?

Dretnor snarled and lunged at me. "You will speak of her with respect. Medusa has abided your cruelty long enough. I will free her from your vile presence, and once I do, she will love me as she promised."

His words startled me enough that I stumbled, and he raked a poisonous claw across the skin of my arm. Ouch, talk about stinging.

Pain didn't stop me from replying, though. "You mean she put you up to this?"

"I tried to discredit you first," said the demon as he stalked me around the bed. "But no one noticed or cared because of your stupid reality show. Then that idiot dragon fell under your spell and helped foil the attack by the assassins."

"And let me guess, you joined the competition to get close to me."

"Yes, but anyone can see the game will be fixed so Drake, your lover, can win. I must make my move now while he is distracted."

"Wait a second," I said, panting as I tried to dodge and still got sliced. The damn chains kept throwing my balance off, and now the poison also made my movement sluggish. "You're the one who called Drake away?"

"I used a cloaked phone and called to tell him we were interested in hiring him to kill you. Loverboy immediately took off to try and save your sorry ass."

My heart melted to know he'd left in an attempt to be my hero. Turned out he should have stayed for more than one reason. "You won't get away with this. All of Hell is watching you right now. Drake will come back any second and eat you. I'm his mate, you know."

"Drake should be dead by now," said Dretnor with a sneer. "His meeting was with a coven of lamia in need of some dragon skin. And you will join him shortly."

"Fucking bastard!" Tears blurred my vision at the thought of Drake dying, and I dove at the demon, uncaring suddenly that I had no weapons to aid me. I just wanted to wrap my hands around his villainous throat and squeeze. But an unarmed, injured half-demon was no match for a full demon running on madness.

He flung me about like a rag doll. I'll admit things weren't looking too good, and I'd run out of options.

Lying on the floor, gasping in pain, my body sporting a multitude of cuts and bruises, I watched Dretnor approach, my impending death in his eyes. I could heal from many things, but the blade he suddenly pulled out made me curse. Even I couldn't recover from a decapitation.

A roar suddenly shook the room, vibrated my skin, and bitch slapped hope back into me.

Could it be?

Dretnor whirled, and I could see, just barely, past one side of him, Drake barreling into the room. But he wasn't Drake for long. Even as my lover moved, his body rippled and grew and grew some more. Scales formed over his skin, ebony-colored pieces that shimmered almost blue when he moved. When he'd finished transforming, a massive dragon crowded the room.

Hot damn.

Steam hissed in and out of Drake's nostrils, and when he spoke—in our heads, not out loud—I shivered at the raw power.

"Step away from my mate. Now."

Intelligence wasn't one of Dretnor's strong points, apparently—just look who he wanted to hook up with

—and instead of obeying something higher up in the food chain, he turned and grabbed me by the hair. I struggled in his grip, but battered and weakened, I didn't accomplish much.

Actually, that wasn't true. If anything, Drake looked even more pissed as he got a better look at the beating I'd received.

"Die," Drake hissed as smoke curled from his nostrils.

Faster than I would have credited a creature of his size, the dragon's forearm lashed out with its razor sharp claws and lopped Dretnor's arm off. Gravity yanked me down. Without Dretnor to hold me up, I expected to meet the floor up close and personal, but Drake, again in a lightning-quick move, grabbed me with his other hand—er, claw.

I found myself tucked under a leathery wing against a gigantic, scaly body, and slumped in relief. And it wasn't just because I'd almost met my maker—if I had one. Drake was alive and safe, not to mention superhot coming to my rescue, even if he was currently a dragon instead of a man.

Dretnor, without his hostage, and minus one arm, didn't look too impressive anymore, but Drake didn't care. His maw, with jagged teeth, opened wide, and he exhaled. A cloud billowed out of his mouth and encased Dretnor, who didn't even have time to say "boo." When the mist cleared, Drake's bedroom had acquired a life-sized ice sculpture of one very ugly demon. Cool.

I might have admired it more, or said something like, "my hero," but I did the most girl thing ever. I swooned.

CHAPTER SIXTEEN

Awareness returned and found me lying on Drake's bed, naked still and spread-eagle, but unbound—what a shame. Raising my head, I looked at my mostly healed body. Wow. How long had I been sleeping?

As if he heard my mental query, Drake answered. "You were out for about twelve hours."

I turned toward Drake's voice and found him standing beside the bed and, even better, completely naked.

"The poison should be out of your system by now, and in another twelve to sixteen hours, the rest of your injuries should be gone."

Thank Satan for super-healing demon blood. I felt like a million bucks considering what had happened, and I wanted to celebrate being alive. What I couldn't understand was why Drake didn't join me on the bed. I could see he wanted me. His cock projected hard enough to do chin-ups on.

I rolled onto my side and smiled at him. "Thanks for killing Dretnor. I guess that makes you the winner. So why don't you come here and show me what a good minion you are?"

He just smiled at me. "Depends. You going to tell me what I want to hear?"

I rolled my eyes. "Are we back to that? Isn't it enough I like fucking you?"

Faster than my half-human eyes could follow, I found myself on my stomach with his deliciously bare body plastered over mine, his throbbing cock pulsing against the crease of my cleft. I wiggled my bottom against him, and he groaned.

"Dammit, baby, you are driving me insane. You are not leaving this bed until you tell me you love me and beg me to mark you."

"Do your best," I said breathlessly. He didn't need to know I intended to cave. I loved him, pure and simple. When I thought he might be dead, I'd suffered more pain than all of my physical injuries put together. But knowing I loved him and secretly wanted him to mark me as his didn't mean I wouldn't really enjoy his attempts to convince me. I'd make sure he worked at it extra hard.

His arm snaked around my waist, and he hoisted my bottom up. When I tried to raise myself on my arms, a heavy hand shoved me down, burying my face into the pillow. Ooh, kinky. His knees nudged my legs apart, and his swollen head rubbed against my already moist lips.

"Are you going to say it?"

"No," I said with a hidden smile.

I yelped at the hard smack he lay on my plump ass cheek, and then I moaned as he followed up with a cock thrust into my tight channel. I'd barely had a chance to clench him when he pulled out and asked again, "Do you love me?"

"Can't we just be friends?" Slap and pump. "Fuck friends?"

Again, he smacked my ass then impaled me. Damn was I having fun. Panting by now, I shook my head when he asked again and bit back my cry as he slapped my already stinging buttocks, but I was ready for the other half of his persuasion, and when he plunged his shaft back in, I tightened my muscles around him.

He grunted as he dug his fingers into my cheeks. "Tell me you love me."

"Not yet," I replied with a hidden grin. This went on for a while. He spanked me and thrust into me, over and over until my ass burned hotly and my pussy even more so. When he threw pinching my clit into the mix, I knew I'd lost the game.

I whispered it. "I love you."

He went still inside of my sexually aching body. "What did you say?"

"I love you, dammit. You and your dragon and your pigheaded, chauvinistic attitude."

He leaned over. and his lips grazed the skin on the back on my neck, sending shivers throughout my body.

"I love you, too, my feisty darling."

I would have replied, but he thrust back into me, and this time, he wasn't fucking around. He pumped me hard and fast, his thick rod finding and striking my G-spot while his hand rubbed at my sensitive clit.

I arched back into him, pushing back against him to drive him in deeper. The coiling pleasure built inside me, feverishly so.

His tempo increased, his cock driving piston-fast into my gripping channel. A low keen emerged as I coasted on the edge of bliss. I felt his lips caress the tender skin of my nape, and when he bit down, I screamed. My orgasm hit me hard as he sank his teeth into me, marking me. And although he didn't speak aloud, I heard him clearly when he said, *Mine*.

A feeling I reciprocated wholeheartedly, even as I almost lost consciousness from the pleasure. He must have come. I didn't know or care, my body too boneless and sated to pay attention. He collapsed on the bed beside me and drew me into the circle of his arms, kissing my temple gently. I burrowed deeper into the warmth of his arms. Sickening, I know, but dammit, it felt so nice I couldn't muster up my usual dislike of such an intimate moment.

"So now what?" I finally asked when my breathing calmed down enough to speak and be understood.

"Now we make love until neither of us can walk."

I giggled. "I was going to do that anyway. I mean this whole mate thing. Seeing as you've marked me, what happens now?"

"I do my best to make you the happiest, most sexually satisfied woman in the world."

"I like that," I murmured. "And as my minion, I also expect coffee, one sugar and two creams, just so you know."

He chuckled, his chest rumbling under my cushioned cheek, and I smiled.

"I wonder what stupid name ended up winning," I said, thanking Satan my contract with the reality show couldn't force me to keep the name the audience had chosen. Imagine being stuck with the name Soul Slut, especially since I was a one-man woman now. And if Drake even thought about not being a one-woman man, he'd be opening himself up to a whole truckload of pain.

"I've got a name for you," he announced suddenly.

"Let's hear it." Although I had to admit, now that he'd bitten me, the title of mate kind of struck my fancy.

He tugged me on top of him, and I looked down at his handsomely rugged face. His eyes glowed in a way I'd come to recognize they only did around me, and his lips curved into the dimpled smile I loved so much. "I think your superhero name should be Wife. And, as your partner, my title will be Husband. What do you say?"

My throat did not close up when I whispered, "That sounds perfect." And it wasn't tears that made my eyes water. *Okay, I'm lying. What can I say? Love does strange things, even to a tough-ass half-demon like me.* Sure, he'd bitten me and all, made me his mate, but marriage, we were talking about public commitment and a chance to go shopping for the wickedest wedding dress ever. *Oh, and let's not forget the shoes.*

EPILOGUE

Last Sidekick Standing proved a resounding success according to the polls, and even more surprising, they unanimously agreed my new title of Wife suited me perfectly—the single females seemed especially happy to crown me with that shackling title. But I didn't mind. I had Drake, and I loved to flaunt him.

To think I'd started my quest looking for a minion to complement me, and instead, I'd found a lover and husband, even if the word husband still made me giggle. But in the end, the whole fiasco had paid off, especially the sex video of Drake and me before the cameras got turned off. We'd be coasting off those sales for years.

As for Medusa, the bitch who started the whole attempts-on-my-life thing, she was currently serving time for a host of crimes, including freeing that nasty

Albert, among other things—Satan was most displeased with her. I sent flowers every week to her jail cell, where she got let out only to clean latrines as part of her punishment. What could I say? If it hadn't been for her jealousy and attacks on my life, I might never have given Drake the chance to show me love wasn't just a bad word.

Life was just about perfect, or would be if Drake would wear the tights and bodysuit I'd gotten for him in his role as my partner for our soul hunting job. But he hadn't lost his stubborn streak, so while I dressed to the nines in various leather outfits, bustiers, and heels, he stuck to his low-hipped jeans with no shirt or shoes. Damned distracting man!

I had my ways to retaliate, though. I'd taken to wearing no panties under my skirts and bending over at crucial moments. It definitely made our jobs more exciting, and it also made for easy access, as there was nothing better than a good, hard victory shag after we'd taken down an escaped soul.

Just thinking about it made me horny. My sex clenched, and moistness made my cleft wet. In a flash, I found myself on my back, Drake above me and, quick as lightning, his cock sheathed in my channel and on a roof in a mortal city no less.

Damn, do I love my randy dragonshifter, the best minion a woman could ever ask for.

THE END

If you enjoyed this twisted version of Hell then you may also enjoy

For even more books with shapeshifters and paranormal freakiness, see EveLanglais.com

www.ingramcontent.com/pod-product-compliance
Ingram Content Group UK Ltd.
Pitfield, Milton Keynes, MK11 3LW, UK
UKHW042001230426
12048UKWH00009B/464